"I thought you knew about Susan's mother," Lila said cautiously, looking first at Caroline, then at Cara. "I mean it's just something I *heard*. It could be a rumor."

"What about her mother?" Caroline asked.

"I really—I shouldn't. . . . I mean, it's none of my business."

"What?"

Lila looked over at Susan and shook her head sadly. "It's not *what*—it's *where*." Lowering her voice, she said, "She's in a hospital for the criminally insane."

Cara and Caroline both gasped. "Are you sure about this?" Cara asked, grabbing Lila by the arm.

An unpleasant sensation of guilt washed over Lila, but she quickly pushed it out of her mind. "Well," she said slowly, "*nobody* really knows anything for sure, do they?"

Then she removed Cara's hand from her arm, stood, and walked away. As she passed by Susan's table she felt a surge of triumph overcoming the guilt. She strode out of the cafeteria with a victorious smile on her face.

Bantam Books in the Sweet Valley High series
Ask your bookseller for the books you have missed

RUMORS

Written by
Kate William

Created by
FRANCINE PASCAL

BANTAM BOOKS

NEW YORK · TORONTO · LONDON · SYDNEY · AUCKLAND

RL 6, IL age 12 and up

RUMORS
A Bantam Book / June 1987

Sweet Valley High is a registered trademark of Francine Pascal

Conceived by Francine Pascal

Produced by Daniel Weiss Associates, Inc.
33 West 17th Street
New York, NY 10011

Cover art by James Mathewuse

ISBN 0-553-27884-3

Published simultaneously in the United States and Canada

Bantam Books are published by Bantam Books, a division of Bantam Doubleday Dell Publishing Group, Inc. Its trademark, consisting of the words "Bantam Books" and the portrayal of a rooster, is Registered in U.S. Patent and Trademark Office and in other countries. Marca Registrada. Bantam Books, 666 Fifth Avenue, New York, New York 10103.

PRINTED IN THE UNITED STATES OF AMERICA

OPM   15 14 13 12 11 10 9 8 7 6

RUMORS

One

"Mom, could you pass the butter, please?"

"Of course, Liz. Here."

Elizabeth Wakefield spread butter on a crisp english muffin and looked back at the front page of the *Sweet Valley News*.

"May I have the comics?"

Without taking her blue-green eyes from the paper, Elizabeth extracted the comics page and passed it to her twin sister.

"Oh, give me a break!" Jessica exclaimed a moment later, licking jam off one finger. "This has got to be the stupidest joke in the whole world. Listen to this: What kind of ghost lives in an easy chair? An upholstergeist."

Alice Wakefield let out a peal of laughter. "Oh, no! Who *writes* jokes like that?"

1

"Sick people," Elizabeth suggested with a lop-sided grin. "People with deranged minds."

Jessica shook her head. "Sick people is right. Say, Mom, when's Dad coming back from Phoenix?"

Mrs. Wakefield lowered her section of the newspaper a fraction and met her daughter's questioning gaze. "Is that a free association with sick people?"

"No! When is he coming, though?"

"Tonight. Why?"

"He said he'd look at the Fiat to see why it's making that weird noise," Jessica explained. The twins shared a red Fiat convertible, and whenever anything threatened to cut off their transportation, it was cause for serious anxiety.

"Well he'll be home by dinnertime, don't worry."

An easy silence descended over the breakfast table in the Wakefields' warm, sunny kitchen. Together, the three Wakefield women made a charming picture: the twins, blond and tanned by the California sun, and their mother, pretty and youthful enough to be taken sometimes for their older sister.

There was no way to miss the fact that the twins were California girls. Although Elizabeth's hair was pulled into a sensible ponytail and Jessica's swung loose and free around her shoulders, it was the same gleaming spun gold, burnished from long hours in the sun. And their trim, perfect size-six figures proved that they spent plenty of time swimming, playing tennis, and jogging. The two girls were identical in every way, down to the dimples in their left cheeks.

Elizabeth's attention was riveted on an article about working mothers; the story was clear, informative, and fair, she decided with a nod of her blond head. Good reporting. If only she could write as well, she wished silently. Elizabeth wrote articles for *The Oracle*, Sweet Valley High's school paper, and hoped to be a professional writer someday. So whenever she could, she liked to read the *News* all the way through.

"It says here that more and more women are choosing not to have any kids at all so they can devote all their time to their careers," she told her mother and sister, shaking her head. "That's a tough choice."

"What a shame," her mother said, frowning. "I enjoy my work, but my family is much more important to me. Much more," she repeated emphatically.

Jessica pulled absently at her delicate gold necklace and sighed. "It must be so much easier to be a man," she said. "You wouldn't have any of those really hard decisions we women have to make all the time."

"Yeah," Elizabeth said wryly. "I know what

you mean. Like which blouse to wear with your new skirt. One of yours or one of mine."

"Ha-ha."

"Listen to this name," their mother said suddenly. "Andrea VanAllen. I think Andrea is just a lovely name."

"Mom! I know who that is," Jessica put in, finishing her orange juice. "She's that rich lady from Bridgewater who's always running charity events and stuff. Mrs. Megabucks." Bridgewater was a town twenty miles away from Sweet Valley and was famous for the number of wealthy people who lived there. It was considered one of the most prestigious areas around.

"Andrea—or Andrew," Mrs. Wakefield continued in a dreamy voice. "They're both nice names."

Jessica pulled the section of paper around so she could read it. "Oh, look. She's in charge of the Bridgewater Ball this year." She met her sister's eyes, and simultaneously they both said, "Whoooa!" and burst into giggles. As identical twins they often said or thought the same thing at the same time. It was only one facet of the special bond they shared.

"The Bridgewater Ball, la-di-da," said Jessica. "You only have to be invited to spend about a million dollars a couple to go. Who needs it?"

Elizabeth grinned. "If you were invited, you

know you'd be out shopping for a new dress within ten seconds, Jess."

"I never said I wouldn't go if I were invited."

"Oh, OK," said Elizabeth, her eyes still twinkling. "I guess I misunderstood you."

Her sister wrinkled her nose and stuck her tongue out at her. "Besides, who wouldn't? I read about it last year after it was over. The theme was 'Mississippi Riverboat,' and they spent something like *five* thousand dollars just on flowers for the Bridgewater Country Club. And they had all these really elaborate ice sculptures, too. One was this giant steamboat made of ice with jumbo shrimp all over it."

"Does it say what this year's theme is?" Elizabeth craned her neck to see over the table.

Jessica quickly scanned the column. "Oh, here it is. 'The theme of the Bridgewater Ball this year will be "Tales from the Vienna Woods." ' Wow, do you think they'll have gondolas and things?"

Mrs. Wakefield chuckled. "Vienna, honey, not Venice. Vienna is Austria. Birthplace of the waltz."

"I knew that."

"All right." The twins' mother stood up and began clearing the table. "But it doesn't look as if you'll get so much as a glimpse. For better or worse, we don't move in such elaborate social circles." She sent Elizabeth a wink as she added,

5

'We're just humble folk in our humble little home.''

Elizabeth knew her mother was kidding. Their home was a comfortable split ranch house with a swimming pool on a quiet street, decorated with her mother's professional touch. She wouldn't trade it for any big mansion. Elizabeth had decided long ago that Sweet Valley, California, was the nicest place in the world to live.

But Jessica pouted. "Well it wouldn't kill us if we lived in a more fashionable part of town, you know. We could have a lot of advantages if we hung out with those people.''

"Like what?'' Elizabeth snorted, amused by Jessica's social ambitions.

"I don't know. But it couldn't hurt. Besides, I bet Dad makes enough money for us to live in a bigger house. Isn't that what lawyers are supposed to do? Make money?''

"Your father just happens to be one of those rare men who practices law because of his convictions, Jessica, not for money.''

Mrs. Wakefield turned from the sink where she had been rinsing dishes, and a grimace of pain crossed her face for a second. She put her hand to her stomach.

"Mom, what is it? What's wrong?'' Elizabeth asked, getting up quickly and coming to her mother's side.

"Nothing, I've just been feeling a little under

6

the weather lately," her mother said hurriedly, a slight frown creasing her forehead. "But that reminds me, I'm going to the doctor this afternoon after work, so I'll be late getting home. I'd appreciate it if you two would make dinner tonight. Your father will be home around six."

Elizabeth and Jessica exchanged a look of concern.

"Mom, are you sure you're OK?" Elizabeth repeated, looking anxiously into her mother's attractive, youthful face.

Mrs. Wakefield smiled and touched Elizabeth's cheek lightly. "I'm fine, sweetheart. Don't worry about me. Now don't you two have to get to school?"

"Oh, no!" Elizabeth said, darting a glance at the wall clock. "I wanted to get to school early to at least get a start on my column."

" 'Bye, Mom."

" 'Bye, Mom. See you later."

Alice Wakefield pushed a stray lock of blond hair behind one ear and smiled at her daughters. "Have a good day, you two. See you tonight."

Pausing only to pick up their books in the hall, Elizabeth and Jessica hurried outside and got into their red convertible. In moments they were driving down their quiet, tree-lined street toward Sweet Valley High.

"I don't hear any weird noise," Elizabeth said to Jessica, who was driving.

"It's when you slow down to stop," Jessica replied. "It sounds like, I don't know—like a buzzing sort of sound."

Elizabeth shrugged and looked at the scenery flashing past. Soon they were pulling up the driveway of the high school, and Jessica turned to her as she switched off the ignition. "What did I tell you? It sounds like the whole car is going to blow up any minute."

"I didn't hear anything, Jess."

"*What?* Are you totally deaf or something? Here, listen." Jessica turned the key, and the engine roared to life again.

By straining her ears, Elizabeth could just make out a faint rattle from under the hood. She chuckled and shook her head. It was typical of her twin to be so dramatic about any tiny noise in the car. That was Jessica, all right. They were identical on the outside, Elizabeth thought, but on the inside they were as different as night and day.

Jessica found drama in everything—or else created it herself, whereas Elizabeth thought of herself as practical and sensible. Half the time she found herself extricating her headstrong twin from some crazy predicament. Jessica never held back on anything, be it her cheerleading or the pursuit of a new boyfriend. It was a more helter-skelter style than Elizabeth liked for herself, but she couldn't imagine her twin any other way. And there was no one in the world who meant more to her than Jessica did.

"You're right, Jess. We'd better get this thing looked at before it kills us both."

Jessica nodded. "See what I mean? I knew something was wrong. Anyway, see you later," she said, springing from the car. Elizabeth opened her door, and the girls hurried into the building to begin their day.

As Elizabeth made her way down the hall, she greeted many of her friends. But when Enid Rollins sent her a wave, Elizabeth just grabbed her best friend by the arm and towed her along.

"Hey! What is this, a hijacking?" Green-eyed Enid laughed.

"Something like that," Elizabeth said, pulling Enid along until they reached the door to the *Oracle* office.

"I haven't finished my column yet," Elizabeth explained with a guilty smile. "Help me, Enid. I'm totally brain-dead today."

The two girls hurried into *The Oracle*'s cluttered office, and Elizabeth sat down at a typewriter. She was the writer of the "Eyes and Ears" gossip column. The column was one of the highlights of the paper, and everyone loved to find themselves and their friends in it, especially because Elizabeth never used her pen spitefully: "Eyes and Ears" was always funny and lighthearted.

But that morning Elizabeth couldn't think of anything at all to write about, and she had to hand in her column by the end of the day.

"Come on, come on, inspire me," she commanded her friend and bit her lower lip with concentration.

Enid laughed, folded her arms, and focused her eyes on the ceiling. "How about—uh, you could write about . . ." Her voice trailed off, and she met Elizabeth's hopeful gaze. "I can't think of anything either."

"Oh, Enid!"

"Well you're the journalist, not me. I don't know how you can think of things to write about every week as it is. And besides," Enid added, flipping through a notebook of past "Eyes and Ears" columns. "There aren't any good events coming up for you to talk about. No big games, no dances—"

"That's it!" Elizabeth shouted, tucking her chair in closer to her desk. "The Bridgewater Ball. I can talk about who might be going."

"Are you serious? It's way over in Bridgewater. What do Sweet Valley High kids want to know about some fancy ball twenty miles away?"

"Some will go, and you know it. Only a few kids from Sweet Valley High will go—that's why it's so juicy." Elizabeth began tapping out the beginning of her column on the typewriter, and Enid looked over to read upside down.

"Well, who do you think will go? Bruce Patman, definitely. His family's so rich, and they always go," Enid said. "So of course that means Regina will go, too."

Elizabeth paused and smiled softly. "I'm glad, aren't you? If anyone deserves to have a good time, it's Regina." Bruce Patman's girlfriend, Regina Morrow, had been born almost totally deaf. She had recently returned from Switzerland where she had undergone extensive treatments, and now she could hear just about perfectly.

Elizabeth thought Regina was a truly special person and had gotten closer to her since the girl's return from Europe. They had spent many hours together talking about the wonderful things Regina had seen and done in Switzerland, and Elizabeth longed to see the beautiful mountains and quaint villages Regina described.

With a nod, Enid agreed. "Regina isn't snobby like a lot of rich people. She's completely sincere. Hmm, I guess Roger Patman will probably go, too," she added, referring to Bruce's half brother.

"Probably," Elizabeth muttered, typing. "And that means he'll take Olivia, so we'll get a good article from her about it. What do you think of

11

this title: 'The Chic Mystique: Who Gets to Go to the Year's Most Exclusive Party?' "

"I love it! I can see it now," Enid said, an impish smile on her face. "A stunning exposé of Sweet Valley's elite set, by ace reporter, Elizabeth Q. Wakefield."

Elizabeth raised one eyebrow. "What's the *Q* for?"

Her friend shrugged. "I don't know. It just sounds good. Hmm. Let's see. I bet Suzanne Hanlon goes. She's about as snobby as they come."

"Oh, please!"

"And how about Lila Fowler? She'll be going, won't she?"

"Probably," Elizabeth said, rolling her eyes. "And I'll never hear the end of it from Jessica. I don't know how those two can say they're best friends when they're always competing with each other. It's pretty bizarre."

Enid made a sour face. "Well, just for once I'd like to see Lila not get the limelight. Wouldn't it kill her if no one asked her to go?"

"Bite your tongue!" answered Elizabeth, suppressing a smile. She glanced down at the two long paragraphs she had just composed and then pulled the piece of paper out of the typewriter with a snap. "A little ego gratification for the lucky few," she quipped, picking up her books. "Ready?"

Enid hopped down from the desk she had been perching on and swung her book bag over her shoulder. "After you, madam."

"Oh, no, no, no!" Elizabeth replied airily. "After you! And I'll see you at the Bridgewater Ball!"

For a moment, Enid's eyes sparkled with mischief. "Let's just see who ends up going. I have a feeling some people would give anything to go to that dance."

Two

Jessica slid into her seat next to Lila in health class and breathed a heavy sigh of resignation. "I didn't do my chemistry homework for today, and Russo called on me. Twice."

"What a drag," Lila drawled, looking around her. "That's the problem with morning classes—you have less time to get the work from someone else first."

"Tell me about it!" Usually she could copy her twin's homework in a pinch, but there were limits even to Elizabeth's generosity.

Jessica glanced quickly to the front of the room: Ms. Rice hadn't arrived yet, so there was still plenty of time to talk. "Look at what Dana's wearing today," she said, nodding her head toward a tall blonde with a wild haircut. "I swear that girl gets more outrageous all the time."

Lila looked over to where Dana Larson sat. She was wearing skintight, leopard-spotted jeans. Dana, the lead singer for a popular band called The Droids, tended to wear eye-catching, new-wave clothes to go with the band's image. But no matter how far-out her wardrobe was, Dana had enough poise to pull anything off. "Where does she buy her clothes?" Lila asked, her voice incredulous.

"Search me. She probably has to go to L.A. for some of them."

"Well, personally, I prefer more sophisticated clothes."

Jessica sighed. Lila Fowler's father was a micro-chip tycoon with a macro-fortune, and he lavished on his daughter everything she could possibly want, including a huge clothing allowance. So Lila was always dressed in the most expensive, elegant things and made sure her appearance was always impeccable. At the moment, she was carefully smoothing her shoulder length, light brown hair with a manicured hand.

"Hmm," Jessica mumbled, making a slightly sour face. Her thoughts went back to her breakfast-table conversation, and she turned to Lila again. "So, are you going to the Bridgewater Ball?"

A slight flush colored Lila's cheeks. "Of course."

16

"Well, who are you going with? That guy Grant?" Recently, Jessica and Lila had made a serious attempt to get boyfriends from Bridgewater. Jessica was positive it was her ticket to the ball. She had dated a boy named Rob Atkins, but that relationship had fizzled out pretty quickly. And Grant Palmer and Lila hadn't turned out to be the romance of the century either.

Lila darted her a quick look. "Well, no one's exactly asked me yet. But I *am* going. The Fowlers always go."

Jessica had a strong desire to make a sarcastic remark, but she managed to suppress it. Lila was one of her best friends, but there were times when Jessica had a hard time dealing with her friend's snobbish attitude. "Well, do you know who else is going?"

"Girls from Whitehead, mostly," Lila answered. Whitehead Academy was the private girls' school in Bridgewater. No one but the most well-to-do went there. "But hardly anyone from Sweet Valley High, of course."

"I bet Susan Stewart is going," Jessica speculated as a tall, graceful redhead took a seat near the front of the room. "With Gordon Stoddard, of course."

"Listen, Jess. *Nobodies* don't go to the Bridgewater Ball."

Jessica stared at Lila, openmouthed. "Nobody's! Come on! Susan probably is a some-body, and you know it. I mean first of all, she lives with that woman who takes care of her, and nobody knows who her mother is, except that she obviously sends a lot of money. Susan wears the most incredible clothes."

"They're OK," muttered Lila, sending a narrow-eyed look up the aisle to Susan Stewart. "If you like that style."

Jessica stared moodily at Susan, too. The girl did wear beautiful clothes—as nice as Lila's—and she had a sense of elegance that made even the plainest things look fantastic. At the moment she was wearing a simple, khaki-colored skirt and a creamy silk blouse that set off her tanned skin and coppery hair beautifully. Her eyelashes and delicately arched brows were a shade darker than her hair, and her wide eyes were a rich, smoky brown.

And on top of it all was the mystery surrounding Susan. Nobody knew who she really was, not even Susan herself. Mrs. Reister, the woman she lived with, had finally agreed to tell her on her eighteenth birthday. But everyone at Sweet Valley High knew Susan couldn't wait that long to find out.

In the meantime, however, a lot of people went out of their way to be friendly to Susan: Jessica thought it was a pretty good idea herself. After all, you never could tell. And besides, she told herself defensively, Susan was really nice.

"I really doubt she'll be going, Jessica. It's really *very* exclusive," Lila added, a slight trace of venom in her voice.

"Well, why don't I just ask her?" Jessica suggested with a sweet, innocent smile that she knew would irritate her friend. Before Lila could stop her, Jessica leaned forward in her seat and called up the aisle to Susan Stewart.

The attractive, redheaded girl turned around with an expectant smile. "Hi, Jessica."

With another quick grin at Lila, Jessica said, "We were just talking about the Bridgewater Ball, and I wondered whether you're going."

Susan nodded. "Yes. I'm going with Gordon and his parents."

As Jessica shot Lila a triumphant look, Maria Santelli, one of Jessica's fellow cheerleaders, gasped. "You're kidding!" she exclaimed, her brown eyes wide with admiration. "That's supposed to be the ritziest social event of the whole year. I can't believe you're actually going."

With a little shrug and a slightly bemused look on her face, Susan said, "Well I don't really know that much about it. All I know is that it's at the country club over in Bridgewater and it has the theme of Old Vienna."

"Only the most important people in Sweet Valley go, you know," Maria continued.

Turning around in her chair, Susan looked back at Lila. "You'll be going, won't you, Lila?"

Jessica glanced quickly at her friend, curious to see how Lila would react. On the one hand, Susan obviously assumed that Lila was one of "the most important people in Sweet Valley." But on the other hand, Lila would have to admit she didn't have a date yet. And a lot of people were following their conversation closely.

"Well . . ."

"Lila, I'll be glad to take you," came a voice from behind them.

Lila turned around swiftly and then rolled her eyes in disgust. "Give me a break, Winston. That's about the stupidest thing I ever heard."

Winston Egbert, the school clown of Sweet Valley High, made a long, comic face, stood up, and walked over to Lila. "But listen, seriously. I've been saving up to buy a car, and I could use the money for tickets instead. No problem."

"Winston, cut it out."

"Lila, please!" he moaned, dropping to his knees in front of her. "Please say you'll go with me to the Bridgewater Ball! I'll do anything! *Anything!*"

"Winston!" Maria gasped, staring at him in mock dismay. "What about me?" Winston and Maria had recently started dating, and Maria was becoming accustomed to his crazy antics.

He brushed her aside with a grand gesture.

"Sorry, Maria. Lila Fowler can get me into a higher social position. That's the breaks. So what do you say, Lila. Is it a date?"

Everyone in the class had turned around to watch Winston teasing Lila, who was rapidly turning a bright shade of pink.

Winston clasped his hands together and looked up at Lila with desperate, pleading eyes. "Listen, if that isn't enough, I could take all the money my parents have saved to send me to college! Please! I'll spend any amount to take you to the Bridgewater Ball! How much are the tickets? Two thousand? Three thousand? Even a million dollars would be a bargain!"

A chorus of laughter made Lila blush even more. Dana shook her head. "Those elitist social events are so bogus. It's just a way for rich people to make themselves feel superior to everyone else."

"You're only saying that because that's the only party around that The Droids aren't asked to play at," Winston said, sending her a fiendish grin.

"Yeah, right!"

"I know!" Winston declared, jumping to his feet. "We can start an annual poor people's ball! Nobody with incomes of more than five hundred dollars a year allowed."

"Speech! Speech!" called Dana, rapping on her desk.

21

Winston assumed an air of modesty, then stood up on his chair. "Thank you. Thank you, everybody. The first annual Poor People's Cotillion will be held in this classroom every February thirtieth from now on. Potato sacks are acceptable dress. Black tie—that means wear shoes with black laces in them—"

"No fair! My sneakers have white laces," Ken Matthews called out, leaning back in his seat and sticking his feet up in the air for inspection.

Winston solemnly regarded Ken's sneakers and shook his head. "You don't qualify. I'm most terribly, terribly, sorry."

"Oh, no!" wailed Ken, burying his face in his hands. "And all I ever wanted was to go to the ball and dance with Winston Egbert."

"Well if that's all you want, why didn't you say so?" Winston jumped down, and while the whole class looked on and laughed, the two boys danced boisterously around the room.

Jessica giggled hysterically as Winston and Ken clowned, and she cast a quick glance at Lila. Her friend's face was rigid with anger, and Lila was darting the most evil looks at Winston. *She can't take a joke at all*, Jessica said to herself.

Finally the two bowed and sat down amid riotous applause, and at that moment Ms. Rice walked in the door. Instant silence descended on the group.

She looked slowly around the room, her eye-

22

brows raised a fraction. Then she glanced at her watch. "Hmm," she said with a sardonic smile. "Remind me not to be late again. I get the feeling the natives have been getting a little restless."

There was a general shuffling of chairs as everyone straightened themselves out and tried to look attentive. Ms. Rice made her way to the front of the class and organized her books and papers.

"All right," she began, sitting down and leaning her arms on the desk. "Yesterday we were talking about human fertility problems and what some people are doing these days to solve them. Do any of you have questions that have been stewing in your hot little minds since then?"

Maria Santelli raised her hand. "Didn't you say that a lot of women have trouble getting pregnant because they wait too long to try and have a baby?"

"Yes, that's one reason for infertility. After a certain age, it becomes more difficult for a woman to conceive."

"Well, I know a woman who had a baby when she was forty-two," Maria went on, a puzzled look on her face. "The normal way," she added.

There was a round of giggles before Ms. Rice could answer.

"That's a very good point, Maria. As I said, some women have more difficulty becoming

23

pregnant after, say, their mid-thirties. But certainly there are women who can and do become pregnant right through their thirties and well into their forties. The human body isn't a machine that works the same way every time. Each one is different."

"Yeah, I read in the *Guinness Book of World Records* that the oldest woman who ever had a baby was something like fifty-seven," Ken said, shaking his head.

Jessica drew her eyebrows together. *Gross,* she thought with a suppressed shudder. She didn't even like the idea of someone in her forties having a baby. Mrs. Wakefield was that old. Jessica shook her head. It was just too unbelievable to think about.

Jessica doodled on the back of her notebook during the rest of the class, not paying much attention. But her ears pricked up at the end of the period when she heard Ms. Rice say the word "quiz."

"What did she say?" Jessica hissed at Lila as they picked up their books and began shuffling toward the door.

"She's giving a quiz tomorrow."

"Oh, God!" Jessica groaned. "I haven't read any of this chapter yet."

"Me either. But come on! How serious can you be about studying for a *health* quiz?" Lila said scornfully.

"My parents are really on my case about get-

24

ting good grades this semester, so that's how serious I can be. I can't *believe* I'm going to have to read this whole thing tonight," Jessica complained, flipping through the pages of her textbook.

Lila shrugged as they entered the crowded, noisy hallway.

"And besides," Jessica continued, raising her voice a little over the noise, "this stuff is too bizarre. Did you hear what she said about how old some women are when they have babies?"

"I know. It's pretty amazing."

Jessica stopped at her locker and began working the combination lock as Lila leaned back, surveying the passing hordes of students. "I mean," Jessica said, "can you imagine someone like my *mother* having a baby? Don't you think that would be pretty ridiculous?"

Lila flipped her hair over her shoulder and shook her head slowly. "I don't know. Your mom isn't all that old—"

"Lila, come on!" Jessica closed her locker door with a snap.

"I bet she could have another baby if she wanted to," Lila went on airily.

"Oh, *please*, Lila, give me a break. No way. And besides," Jessica continued as they started walking again, "why would my mother want any more kids? I think she should be pretty satisfied with the ones she's got."

"Well, wouldn't you like to have another brother or sister?" Lila asked, her brown eyes sincere for once.

Jessica shrugged again. She knew Lila had always wished for a brother or sister. Being an only child must be pretty lonely, she realized with a pang of sympathy for her friend. *Where would I be without Liz?* she thought, shaking her head. *Or Steven, for that matter,* she added, thinking about her older brother, a freshman in college. But on the other hand, her mother had a successful career as an interior designer. Why should she give that up to have a baby when she already had three kids?

"Hi, Jessica! Hi, Lila," someone yelled.

Jessica flashed a brilliant smile as a group of boys passed them, then went on in a lower voice, "No," she repeated. "It's out of the question."

"If you say so."

"I say so. There's no way my mother would ever have any more kids."

Three

"Good try, Mrs. Stoddard. You almost got out of the sand that time." Susan Stewart smiled encouragingly at the older woman, who scowled at the golf ball at her feet.

"Now, partner, don't egg on the competition," Mr. Stoddard, a florid-faced senior vice president at West Coast OilCam Corporation said. He narrowed his light blue eyes and spoke sternly to his wife. "Same thing you do every time, Binky. You're not following through."

Mrs. Stoddard darted a quick look at her husband and pressed her lips together. "Richard has been working on my swing, dear. I'm just trying to hold my arms the way he told me to."

"Well, that pro hasn't been working hard enough," the man shorted, giving his son and Susan a broad wink.

*"Dar-*ling!" Mrs. Stoddard gave the three a tight smile and faced her ball again.

As Gordon's mother waved her iron and tried to align her shoulders, Susan restrained a sigh and looked out across the fairway. The Sweet Valley Country Club was a rolling expanse of manicured green, with a winding brook and duck pond between the seventh and eighth holes. Mrs. Stoddard always got stuck there.

But the sun was shining from a beautiful, clear sky, and a light, tangy breeze carried the scent of the nearby Pacific with it. So it was hardly a sacrifice, Susan told herself with a little smile. She could be in worse places than at the exclusive club for the afternoon.

She glanced at Gordon and smiled softly. He was so sophisticated. Tall, athletic-looking, and handsome, Gordon Stoddard had the kind of polished attractiveness Susan saw in lots of wealthy people. His features were finely molded and aristocratic, and he had keen blue eyes and glossy light brown hair.

"Your shot, Susan."

"Oh, excuse me," she said with a brilliant smile. She patiently waited while Mr. Stoddard told her exactly how to stand and how to swing and then let loose with a clean, clear shot down the middle of the green. Her ball rolled slowly to a stop within a few feet of the eighth hole.

"Excellent shot, Susan. I told you that grip would help you out."

Turning to her left, Susan caught Gordon's eye, and he gave her a slight, mischievous smile from behind his father's back. She lowered her head quickly to hide her own grin.

"You play the game very well, Susan," her boyfriend murmured in her ear.

She chuckled and looked into his clear blue eyes. "Which game is that?"

"I don't understand why I can't do it that way," Mrs. Stoddard complained, patting her beautifully styled, light brown hair with a be-jeweled hand as she watched her husband make a long, clean drive. "I don't think I'll enter the club tournament after all."

They climbed into the golf cart and rolled quickly down to the green. The cart was just like the club, Susan thought: Quiet, well oiled, and expensive.

"I don't know about the tournament anyway, Bink," Mr. Stoddard was saying, his voice a gruff rumble. "They're letting all kinds of people in lately. I think the membership of this club has really deteriorated in the past year or so. It just wasn't what it used to be. I say it's a good thing we joined the membership committee when we did."

"Oh, dear, I really—"

"And not just the club, you know," he went

on, cutting off his wife's protest. "The whole town! Used to be you didn't find any riff-raff anywhere near Sweet Valley. Just the right kind of people, that's how it started out."

Mrs. Stoddard nodded sadly. "You might have a point, Farley, dear. We've been getting applications to the Junior League from some very unsuitable people."

"Hmmph. The right kind of people," Mr. Stoddard repeated with a terse nod as he stopped the cart. He frowned as he reached for an iron, but his face cleared as he looked at Susan, and he winked. "The right kind of people, Susan. *Your* kind of people. *Our* kind of people."

She smiled and swallowed while she tried to think of something to say. *Am I the "right kind of people"?* she asked herself with a rare surge of anxiety. *Am I really the daughter of someone important?*

As Gordon's parents bickered over Mrs. Stoddard's grip, Susan and Gordon stolled away a few paces.

"I guess you think my parents are kind of hung up on that stuff," Gordon began uncertainly, giving her a strained smile.

She shrugged. "I don't mind, I guess. That's just the way they are. I understand." With a tender smile she took Gordon's hand in hers and looked up into his eyes. "I know you'd still like me even if I weren't the 'right kind of people.' "

For a moment he hesitated and dropped his eyes from hers while a slight flush showed through his tan. Then he laughed hollowly. "Sure. Sure I would. Hey, you know that's a really nice outfit you've got on. It's new, isn't it?"

Susan glanced down at the pink-and-white golf skirt and blouse she was wearing and nodded. "Yes. I couldn't face the idea of showing up here another day in that same old thing I've been wearing. Isn't that terrible?" she added, her beautiful face lighting up with a breezy laugh.

"Kids! Gordon, it's your play!"

He squeezed her hand. "Come on. If we're lucky we'll reach the eighteenth hole by sometime tomorrow morning."

"Please!" She giggled, but her brow furrowed for a moment. "Actually I do have to do some studying tonight. I have a stupid health quiz tomorrow. Are your parents planning to stay for dinner?"

With a grimace, Gordon nodded, and some strands of his light brown hair fell into his eyes. "When don't they?" he asked as she gently brushed it aside.

"Susan, darling," Mrs. Stoddard said to her as they rejoined the adults. "We've just been talking about the Bridgewater Ball. I'm so glad you'll be joining us," she added, with a pointed look at her son.

"I'm very excited about it, Mrs. Stoddard. And I was wondering if you could suggest what I should wear?"

"Well . . ." Binky Stoddard glowed visibly at Susan's request for advice and put one finger to her lips in concentration. "Long, of course. And really, I think pale gold is your best color. And so suitable for a young girl of your age. Don't you think so, dear?"

Her husband grunted, shifted his feet, and took a few practice swings.

"Yes—and a bunch of tiny rosebuds, Gordon. That's what you should bring her as a corsage. White rosebuds with just a hint of blush on them."

"Yes, Mother."

"How about a little less talk and a little more golf, hmm?" Mr. Stoddard called out peevishly, looking back at the group with a scowl.

"Yes, dear. Susan," Mrs. Stoddard continued in a lower voice, "the garden club is having a new members meeting on Saturday morning and I think you ought to come along—see what we're all about."

Susan stifled a little groan and managed a smile. "Thanks very much, Mrs. Stoddard. That would be wonderful."

Later on she was able to let her mind wander as they sat through a delicious and opulent dinner in the club's dining room. Mr. Stoddard talked nonstop throughout the meal about his conviction that Sweet Valley was going to the dogs and that they would all be murdered in their beds if the police didn't start to shape up. It was a speech Susan had heard so often she almost knew it by heart. She knew when to nod and when to voice sympathetic agreement. But she found it somewhat offensive and more than a little tedious.

It was wonderful to eat at the club, however, and she decided it was worth listening to her boyfriend's father. *If this is what having social status means,* she mused, looking around her at the well-contented, well-fed members, *then I like it. Everyone is happy, confident. No worries.* She quickly pushed aside her own anxieties about losing it all: What if her mother wasn't famous and rich?

With a resolute decision not to worry about anything, she relaxed and enjoyed the rest of the dinner. Finally, Mr. Stoddard's monologue petered out, and just before they got up to go, Lila Fowler and her father, George, stopped by their table.

"Farley! Bink! Coming to the membership committee meeting tomorrow night?"

Mr. Stoddard nodded his head emphatically.

"You'd better believe it, George. And let me tell you . . ."

As the three adults discussed an "unsuitable" candidate for membership, the three teenagers looked at one another uncomfortably. Susan knew Gordon and Lila had dated several times, and she had the distinct feeling that Lila was not exactly a fan of hers.

"I noticed you finally got a new golf outfit, Susan," Lila said sweetly. "It's so cute."

"Thanks," she answered coolly. Susan cast a quick glance at Gordon, who was fussing with his napkin. He wasn't going to help, she realized disappointedly.

"Do you have a date yet for the ball?" she asked, unable to think of anything else to say.

It was a mistake. Lila's eyes narrowed and she drew her breath in sharply. *"Not yet,"* was the stiff reply.

Another awkward silence enveloped them, and to Susan's great relief, George Fowler turned to his daughter and took her arm. "Let's get going, honey. I've got some papers to look over at home. Good night, everybody."

The Stoddards and Susan stood up themselves, and before long they were on the way home.

"Good night, and thank you very much for dinner," Susan said, stepping out of the Stoddards' red Mercedes.

34

"I'll walk you to the door."

Gordon got out with her, and together they walked up the path to the modest bungalow-style house that Susan Stewart called home.

"About this afternoon—" Gordon began, casting a glance out to the car. He turned and met her gaze. There was a troubled expression in his eyes.

"Yes?"

He bit his lip. "Well, I just hope you don't think my parents are too—well, you know . . . " His voice trailed off. He was obviously uncomfortable.

"Gordon, I don't care, I really don't," Susan assured him, the corners of her mouth twitching slightly. "Your parents might be a little snobbish, but it doesn't really bother me. So don't worry about it, OK? OK?" she repeated, trying to cajole a smile from him. She smoothed the lapels of his well-tailored navy blazer and met his eyes.

A wide grin of relief broke over his handsome, aristocratic features. "OK. Good night." He leaned over and kissed her lightly. Then he trotted down the walkway and climbed into the car. The Mercedes rolled away noiselessly and disappeared around the corner.

With a contented sigh, Susan turned and opened the door. As she stepped into the house, Mrs. Reister, an attractive but anxious-looking woman raised her eyes from the sewing in her lap. She gave Susan a warm, welcoming smile. "Hello, Susan. Did you have fun this evening?"

"Hi, Aunt Helen," the girl answered, throwing herself down onto a cozy, overstuffed couch. "I had a wonderful time."

Mrs. Reister put down the dress she was hemming. "Tell me all about it," she said eagerly. "You know how much I love to hear about what you do."

"Well, we played golf, of course."

"Did Mrs. Stoddard choke up on the eighth hole?"

Susan chuckled and ran a hand through her hair. "Of course! Oh, and Aunt Helen," she added, rolling over onto her side to look into the older woman's eyes, "what do you think of pale gold for my ball dress? Wouldn't that be nice?"

"I think it would be perfect," Mrs. Reister said, nodding slowly.

Mrs. Reister's brow furrowed for an instant, deepening the fine worry lines around her gentle brown eyes; but the frown quickly disappeared. "I was wondering," she continued haltingly. "I designed a dress—just a sketch—only if you like it, of course. Otherwise, we could buy you one."

"Oh, let me see!"

With a look of obvious relief, Mrs. Reister

pulled out a sheet of paper with a series of sketches on it. She handed it to the girl silently.

"Ohhh . . ." Susan murmured, shaking her head. She raised her luminous brown eyes to Mrs. Reister's face. "This is *beautiful*. And I know you can do it, too. You sew so well."

"Well I'll only make it if you really want it, Su—"

"I do! And it would look so fantastic in gold. I know it would!" Susan was filled with eager anticipation as she pictured herself in the long, flowing gown with a fitted waist, dropped shoulders and elegant, plunging back.

Susan pursed her lips for a moment and held the sketch up. "You know, this would look great on you, too, Aunt Helen. You have the same coloring as I do. How come you never make anything really nice for yourself?"

A light flush colored Mrs. Reister's face, and she stood up quickly and went to the window. "You know I never go anywhere, Susan. I get enough pleasure just hearing all about the wonderful parties and things you get invited to. Besides," she added, turning around with a light laugh, "I'm just too busy."

Busy working all the time, Susan realized with a twinge of guilt. *But why?* she wondered for the hundredth time. *If my real mother sends money, why does Aunt Helen have to work so hard?*

She had always understood that Mrs. Reister

took care of her because, for some reason, her real mother couldn't admit to having a child. Countless hours had gone by while she speculated on her past. Had Mrs. Reister been the trusted servant of some rich, unmarried girl who got into trouble? Or maybe Susan was the product of a tragic love affair, entrusted to Mrs. Reister until the truth could be revealed. Maybe— *always maybe*!

There was just no way to know, because Mrs. Reister, usually the warmest and most generous of people, absolutely refused to tell Susan the real story. At least until her eighteenth birthday.

"I have to get ready to go to work," Mrs. Reister said, breaking into Susan's thoughts."

"What? It's so late, though!"

"I know, but I had a chance to put in some extra hours at the restaurant, so I thought I'd take advantage of the opportunity."

As Mrs. Reister hurried out of the room, Susan stared blankly at the floor. Working as a waitress was exhausting for her guardian, but she never complained about long hours and tired feet. And to make extra money, Mrs. Reister also worked as a seamstress at home.

Often Susan had wondered what her life would be like if her aunt Helen *were* her real mother. It would be wonderful to finally have a mother—someone like Aunt Helen: warm, loving, understanding. Whenever she thought of what a mother should be, she always pictured the kindhearted woman who had raised her from infancy.

But of course, her life wouldn't be the same if she had a waitress as a mother. People wouldn't treat her as well as they did, and she wouldn't have the advantages she did now. She wouldn't be invited to go to the Bridgewater Ball or to play golf or any of the other great things she was asked to do with Sweet Valley's elite social set.

No, she told herself regretfully. *I wouldn't be where I am today if Aunt Helen were my real mother. Nothing would be the same at all.*

Four

"Ahhh! I'm pooped!" Ned Wakefield leaned back on the sofa and put his feet up on the coffee table. Turning his head sideways he regarded his wife with his intelligent brown eyes. "And another great dinner, sweetheart."

Alice Wakefield chuckled. "You're just easy to please, that's all. And besides, I wasn't the cook tonight."

"Oh, no? Who was, Liz?"

"No, I was!" Jessica protested, feeling slightly hurt. "You know meat loaf is my specialty."

Her father leaned forward and tweaked her nose. "Sorry, Jess. I forgot. It was delicious."

"Thanks."

Jessica and her parents were in the comfortable living room. Immediately after dinner Elizabeth had gone out with her boyfriend, Jeffrey

French, and Jessica was feeling bored. She also felt nervous and uneasy for some reason and wished her sister were home to talk to.

As her parents turned on the television, Jessica sighed and looked down at the textbook in her lap. There were a lot of things she would rather be doing than studying for her health quiz, but there was no way around it. With another heavy sigh, she opened her book and began reading.

"Did you go to see Dr. Quentin this afternoon?" she heard her father say in a low voice.

She glanced up to see her mother nod and put a finger to her lips. Jessica cocked her head to one side, perplexed at her mother's secrecy. Down on the floor, a handsome golden retriever puppy looked up at her, as if asking for an explanation. She met Prince Albert's eyes, and for a moment she thought about asking her mother what the doctor had said but then decided against it. She shrugged, and the dog put his head down on his paws. She went back to her studying.

"As the hormone levels change, feelings of irritability are not uncommon. Some women claim to have cravings for unusual foods," Jessica read.

Repressing another sigh of boredom, Jessica continued to take notes, keeping half an ear on the TV program her parents were watching.

Suddenly Alice Wakefield turned to her husband. "Ned, do we have any ice cream?"

He looked taken aback. "I don't think so."

"I want some ice cream. I'd really love some ice cream right now. Pistachio."

"Pistachio? You want pistachio ice cream?"

A stubborn look crossed Mrs. Wakefield's face. "Yes. What's wrong with wanting pistachio ice cream?"

"Well, I've just never in my whole life seen you eat pistachio ice cream, that's all."

Jessica followed this conversation with increasing concern. Her mother's voice was sharp, and her arms were crossed obstinately. Suddenly Jessica's blue-green eyes widened, and she looked back at the passage she had just copied into her notebook. It was as if she had just put the last piece of a puzzle into place and saw what the picture was. Doctors? Talking about favorite names? Cravings? She swallowed hard. Could her mother be pregnant?

"Honey, I'm too tired to go out and get ice cream tonight. Can't you eat something we've already got in the house?"

"Oh, Ned!" With an angry cry, Mrs. Wakefield pushed herself up off the couch and stalked from the room. "I'm going out for pistachio ice cream!" she called from the hallway.

The kitchen door slammed.

Jessica stared speechlessly at her father, who looked steadily at the television. Prince Albert raised his head and whined softly. Jessica swallowed with difficulty.

"Dad, is—"

"I think I'll go look over my case notes for tomorrow," he said, cutting her off. He stood up and stretched, then threw her a little smile. "I'll be in my study, Jess."

"Sure, Dad."

The words on the page in front of her blurred as Jessica tried to focus her thoughts. Pregnant! How could that be?

Jessica lifted one eyebrow and tapped the book on her lap. It was pretty obvious *how*, she told herself. But *why*?

Get a grip on yourself, she commanded herself severely. *Mom couldn't be pregnant. Examine the facts*. With a rare burst of organization, Jessica pulled out a sheet of paper and began making a list.

"One: Mom went to the doctor today because she's been feeling sick in the mornings. Two: She didn't want to hear when Dad asked her about it. Three: She's got cravings." Jessica shuddered slightly as she thought about pistachio ice cream. Under normal circumstances, *nobody* in her house wanted pistachio ice cream.

She put the tip of her pencil to her lips and looked at the dog. "Four: She got all weird this morning talking about the names she likes. Five: She's irritable."

Jessica quickly reread her list, hoping she would discover a perfectly logical reason why all those things would be true. The only perfectly logical reason she could think of was that Mrs. Wakefield was expecting a baby.

The front door opened and closed quietly, and Elizabeth poked her head into the living room. "Hi, Jess."

"*Liz!*"

Frantically picking up her books, Jessica raced across the room and grabbed her sister's arm.

"Jess—!"

"*Shhh!*" Jessica clamped her hand over Elizabeth's mouth and darted a quick glance across the hall to the closed door of her father's study. "Upstairs," she hissed, dragging her sister toward the stairs and ignoring her twin's muffled protest.

Halfway up the steps she took her hand from Elizabeth's mouth but shook her head with an urgent warning to be silent.

"Jessica, would you please—"

"In here." Jessica pushed open the door of her room and stopped briefly on the threshold, looking for a clear space to put down her books. "The Hershey Bar," as Jessica's room was nicknamed because of the dark brown walls, was a permanent disaster zone. Jessica's methods of housekeeping were extremely free-form, and she was known to lose items of clothing for weeks at a time.

With an impatient gesture, she swept a pile of laundry from her bed and sat down, pulling Elizabeth with her. "Look at this," she commanded, thrusting her list into her sister's lap.

Elizabeth gave her a skeptical look but finally turned her eyes to the list and scanned it quickly. She looked back at Jessica. "What is this?"

"Don't you see?"

"See what, Jessica? I don't know what you're getting at."

"Liz, how can you be so blind! Here, read this." Jessica opened her health textbook to the passage about cravings in pregnant women and handed it triumphantly to her twin.

Elizabeth frowned, and she raised serious eyes to Jessica's. "Are you thinking what I think you're thinking?"

"If you're thinking what I'm thinking, you're thinking the same thing."

"Ugh!" Elizabeth shook her head impatiently. "We sound like a vaudeville act, Jess. Are you trying to say you think Mom is pregnant?"

"Yes!"

"But, Jessica, that's ridiculous!"

"And why is it so ridiculous?" Jessica demanded, folding her arms across her chest.

Elizabeth opened her mouth to speak and

then shut it with a snap. "Because it is, that's all," she finally said with a weak smile.

"Well, what about all this? Can you think of a reason for all these things? Anything that would tie them all together?"

There was a long pause. "Well, no, but—"

Jessica grabbed her twin's hand. "Listen, has she said or done anything else lately that you didn't think about at the time but that would make sense if she's having a baby? Anything?"

Elizabeth thought for a moment while Jessica watched her closely. "Actually," she said, her voice reluctant, "actually, a couple of days ago I was toasting some english muffins. . . ."

"Yeah?"

"Oh, Jess! It's too dumb. It didn't mean anything."

Standing up, Jessica faced her sister and put her hands on her hips. "Elizabeth, this is very important. What about the english muffins?"

"Well, Mom just said something like, it was such a pain having everything come in packages of six when there are five of us in the family, because there's always one left over. She said families with four kids were better off because they didn't have to fight over who got the last muffin."

"See? You see? *Four kids!* She wants to have another kid!"

Thinking, Elizabeth picked up a silk scarf from

47

the floor and began drawing it back and forth between her hands. Finally she looked up. "Why don't we just ask her, Jess?"

"Ask her? Ask her? Are you crazy?"

"Why not?"

"Oh, God!" Jessica whirled around and stalked to the window. "Don't you see how secretive she's being about it? I mean, if she wanted us to know, wouldn't she tell us?"

Elizabeth said nothing.

"Come on, Liz. Wouldn't she?" Jessica looked at her twin and tapped her foot.

Slowly Elizabeth nodded. "I guess you're right. But how can we know for sure?"

A quick smile flashed over Jessica's face. "Well, I think in a case like this we have every right to spy on her."

"Jessica!" Elizabeth exclaimed, her expression disapproving.

"Well, we do! I mean, it's not as if she were just planning to buy a new refrigerator or something. We're talking about *our* little brother or sister."

The expression on Elizabeth's face changed suddenly from disapproval to wonder. "A little baby," she said softly. "Gosh, can you imagine?"

Jessica's whirling thoughts slowed down for a moment as the idea slowly sank in. In all her chaotic speculating, she hadn't really considered what the *result* of her mother's being pregnant would be. A new brother or sister in the family. A whole new little person. A baby.

"Wow," she said slowly, shaking her head. Her eyes met Elizabeth's, and they looked at each other in awed silence.

Slowly a grin broke over Elizabeth's face, and Jessica felt herself starting to smile, too. Elizabeth gripped her twin's hand, her eyes shining. "Jess!" she breathed. "Oh, can you believe it!"

"I can't believe it!" Jessica shrieked suddenly, bouncing forward to hug her twin. "I can't believe it!"

Elizabeth pressed one hand to her lips and tried to be calm for a moment. "Now let's just wait a minute. We don't know for *sure*."

"Oh, Liz! How can you . . ."

"We don't know for *sure*," Elizabeth repeated firmly, looking sternly at her twin. Her serious expression dissolved as she broke into a wide grin again, however. "So we've got to *make* sure."

Jessica looked searchingly into her sister's eyes. Long ago, Jessica had learned to trust her twin's judgment when it came to really important things, and this definitely qualified as "really important." "What should we do?"

"Just what you said," Elizabeth answered, grinning widely. "We've got to spy on her. But carefully!" she added as Jessica started to speak.

Jessica looked offended and crossed her arms

49

defiantly. "Elizabeth Wakefield, are you forgetting that sneaking around is what I do best?"

Elizabeth laughed. "Oh, Jess, you're too much."

"Yeah, I guess I am, huh?"

Jessica drew a deep breath and looked around the messy bedroom. Scattered here and there among the clothes were some of her mother's things she had borrowed at various times in the past and not returned. It was always a good idea to have an excuse in case you got caught, she told herself.

"I'll just put all of Mom's clothes back in her closet one afternoon this week," she said with a mischievous grin. "And if I happen to see anything while I'm in her room, well, that's not my fault, is it?" She turned innocent eyes to her sister, and they both burst into giggles.

"OK, and we should sound her out a little bit—you know, talk about babies and big families and stuff. Casually."

Jessica nodded. "Subtle. We've got to be subtle."

Her twin snorted. "You're usually about as subtle as a hand grenade, Jessica."

"Please. Give me a little credit for knowing how to spy, Liz. This'll be the best performance of my life."

Suddenly Elizabeth sobered, and she shook her head. "It'll have to be, Jess."

Five

"Hi, Liz," came a quiet voice from somewhere above Elizabeth's right shoulder.

She turned around and found Allen Walters standing in back of her in the long lunch line. She gave the tall boy a sunny smile.

"Hi, yourself," she said, looking up at him. "Take any good pictures lately?"

With a shy grin, Allen nodded. Whenever he took a break from his science club projects, Allen spent his time behind his camera. For all his height, he seemed to be able to make himself unobtrusive, and he usually ended up taking revealing and sensitive candid shots. His photographs were a popular feature of *The Oracle*.

The line moved forward slowly, and Allen shifted a big calculus textbook from one arm to the other. "I was at the game with Big Mesa yesterday. I think some of the pictures I got of the guys on the beach will be OK."

"OK?" Elizabeth shook her head and looked up into his open, honest face. "Allen, you know they'll be great."

He blushed, the color spreading rapidly over his cheeks, and smiled hesitantly. "Well, I do get good shots sometimes," he admitted in a quiet voice. He met her teasing smile and blushed again.

"Oh, Allen." She fingered the gold lavaliere hanging from a chain around her neck and tried to look stern. "It's not a crime to be proud of yourself, you know."

"Well, I—" He broke off suddenly, staring at the door. Although it seemed impossible, he blushed even deeper.

Surprised, Elizabeth followed his gaze. Several girls were talking and laughing by the door, and in the center of the group stood Susan Stewart. Allen was staring at her with an unmistakable look of adoration.

Elizabeth's eyes widened, and she looked from Allen to Susan and back again. There was no way the boy could hide what he was feeling. Allen obviously had a huge crush on the stunning redhead, and Elizabeth couldn't resist a smile. He used to date Robin Wilson, co-captain of the cheerleading squad, and he had taken it pretty hard when she broke up with him. Elizabeth was happy that he had finally gotten over her. She wished, though, that Allen would get interested in some girl who didn't already have a boyfriend. Still, Susan would be a good friend for Allen.

"I bet you could take some great photos of Susan," she said lightly, her eyes on his face.

"N-no," he stammered. There was a hopeless, stricken look in his eyes. "No, I couldn't."

"Why not?" Elizabeth pressed him, tilting her head to one side. "You should just ask her. I bet she'd be really flattered."

"No—I—she's too—I mean, I'm just nobody," he finished lamely, casting a forlorn glance in Susan's direction.

"But that's dumb, Allen," Elizabeth said. "You're definitely a somebody. And Susan isn't a snob or anything."

"Of course she isn't," he retorted swiftly. His voice was intense as he continued. "She's too good a person to be a snob, no matter who she is."

Elizabeth said, "Maybe you should just ask her, Allen. Besides, just because she has a boyfriend doesn't mean you can't be friends."

But he shook his head violently. "No, she wouldn't want to bother with a guy like me." He stopped suddenly, looking at Elizabeth, and the color spread over his face again. He looked quickly away.

Elizabeth realized that this tall, quiet boy would never have spoken so openly about his feelings under normal circumstances. But he obviously felt so strongly about Susan that he couldn't stop himself. And now he was clearly sorry for revealing so much.

"Well, maybe she'd surprise you," she said gently. "Give her a chance."

Allen sent her a look of gratitude and relief, but he still shook his head. "No, I'll just—"

"Hi, Liz. Hi, Allen."

He whirled around and found Susan standing beside him. The blush washed over his features again, but Susan didn't seem to notice.

"Hi, Susan," Elizabeth said, darting a quick look at Allen. He appeared to be completely tongue-tied.

But Susan was looking up at him, a friendly, trusting smile on her face. "Allen, could you explain what Mr. Rizzo was saying about catalysts yesterday in class? I'm really confused."

At the word "catalyst" Allen relaxed visibly. If there was one thing he could talk about with ease, it was science—any schoolwork, in fact. Being an ace student was something he did take pride in. He paused for a moment, considering. Then he gave Susan a brief, simple explaination.

Susan raised her eyebrow when he was done. "Is that all?"

With a bashful smile, Allen shrugged. "That's it."

"Well, why couldn't Mr. Rizzo just say that?" She chuckled, shaking her head so her coppery hair swung back. She threw Elizabeth a grin. "Maybe Allen should be the treacher, and Rizzo can go retire."

Elizabeth smiled. "Allen has a lot of hidden talents," she said casually. "There's a lot more there than meets the eye."

"Oh, I'm sure that's true!" Susan said with an easy laugh. She put her hand on Allen's arm for a moment. "Thanks a lot, Allen. You're a lifesaver."

"No—no problem," he stammered, reduced to near speechlessness by her touch.

"Well, see you later. 'Bye."

Elizabeth watched thoughtfully as Susan made her way through the crowded cafeteria, answering the greetings of her many friends. She seemed to be as friendly and open with everyone else as she was with Allen, so it didn't look as though she thought of Allen as anything more than a friend.

Finally Elizabeth found herself at the front of

the line, and she picked up a chicken salad plate to put on her tray. Her thoughts strayed back to Susan, and she shook her head. *She doesn't know what she's missing,* she told herself silently. She picked up a carton of milk and slid her tray down to the cashier.

"See you later," she said to Allen.

He looked down at her, a slightly wistful smile on his face. "Yeah. 'Bye, Liz."

She paused for a moment, but then she caught sight of Regina Morrow and hurried over to speak with her. Regina always fascinated Elizabeth with stories of her stay in Switzerland. She especially loved to hear about the wonderful boarding schools they had there. Although Regina had had a private tutor while she was in Switzerland, she had several friends in exclusive Swiss boarding schools. The more Elizabeth heard, the more intrigued she became, and she had a lot of questions for Regina. She knew it was ridiculous to even think of going to one of those schools. But it sounded so wonderful, she just had to know more.

Lila idly twirled the straw in her can of Diet Coke and watched Susan Stewart take a seat a few tables away. She narrowed her eyes and made a sour face.

"Lila, are you deaf or something?"

"What?" she snapped back at her friend Cara Walker. "I didn't hear what you said, OK?"

Cara tipped her head back slightly and gave Lila a skeptical look. "All I said was, have you noticed how bizarre Jessica's acting today?"

"No," Lila answered flatly, picking up a carrot stick and munching on it.

"I guess Jessica isn't the only bizarre one today," muttered Cara. "But anyway, I was waiting for her to come to lunch, and she said she was going to the library to read some kind of medical book or something. Don't you think that's pretty strange?"

Lila smiled wryly. "You mean for Jessica to study during lunch? Yes. And for that matter," she continued in a sarcastic tone, "I didn't even know she knew where the library was." She resumed her careful observation of Susan Stewart and unconsciously frowned.

"Mmm," Cara mumbled. "Well I just hope it isn't something about Steve," she added. Steven Wakefield and Cara had been dating steadily for some time. "Oh, great. Here comes Caroline Pearce."

As the red-haired girl came toward them, Lila breathed a heavy sigh. She'd had enough of redheads already. Besides, Caroline used to be one of the biggest gossips at Sweet Valley High, and even though she had recently "reformed" she still liked to "talk," as she put it. Lila wasn't in the mood for talking at the moment.

"Hi," Caroline said breathlessly, setting her tray down on the table. "What a zoo."

"Hmm," Lila answered. She still concentrated on Susan.

"What's wrong with Jessica?" Caroline asked Cara as she opened a bag of Doritos. "She was really weird this morning when I saw her."

"I don't know. I think she's going through some kind of studying phase."

As Cara and Caroline talked, Lila kept her gaze fixed on Susan Stewart, who was deep in conversation with Gordon Stoddard. *Who does she think she is, anyway?* Lila fumed internally. *Just because her mother is supposed to be some mysterious famous person . . . She needs to be taught a lesson.*

Cara's voice intruded on her thoughts, and Lila focused her attention on the two girls sitting across from her. Cara was a reformed gossip, too, just like Caroline. But if there was something—something *really* big, really *juicy*— Lila knew they'd be *un*reformed pretty fast. No doubt about it.

"I think it's so sad, don't you?" she said, casually wiping her mouth with a paper napkin.

Caroline's green eyes widened slightly, and

Cara paused with her sandwich halfway to her mouth. "What is?" Caroline asked slowly.

"About Susan Stewart. Don't you think it's awful?"

Carefully putting down her sandwich, Cara drew a deep breath. "What about Susan Stewart?"

Lila's face registered alarm and surprise, and just a touch of hesitation. "Oh," she faltered, looking from one to the other. "I—I thought you knew."

As Caroline turned around in her chair to look for Susan among the crowded tables, Cara stared at her friend. "Knew *what*, Lila?" she pressed, her voice low.

"Yeah, what?" echoed Caroline, her eyes glowing with eagerness.

"I really—I shouldn't. I thought you both . . ." Lila shook her head and raised a hand to push back her light brown hair. "I mean, it's none of my business. . . ."

"Lila, would you just tell us what you're talking about?" Cara demanded sternly.

Lila hesitated for another moment, then decided to plunge in all the way. "Well," she said, leaning forward across the table, "I heard she found out who her mother is, and it's, well—"

She broke off dramatically, taking stock of the reaction she was producing. Cara and Caroline were practically climbing across the table with curiosity. Just as she had expected.

Caroline brushed aside a lock of straight red hair with an impatient gesture. "What—I mean who—?"

Lila toyed with her straw for a moment, then looked up again. "It's not *who*. It's *where*." She lowered her voice as she added, "In a hospital for the criminally insane."

A shocked gasp escaped from both girls, and they craned their necks to look across the room at Susan.

"Are you *serious*?" Cara hissed, her dark brown eyes wide.

Before answering, Lila hesitated delicately. "I can't swear it's true," she admitted cautiously, meeting Caroline's eyes. "I mean it's just something I *heard*. It could be a rumor."

"But what was she supposd to have done?"

"I—I don't really know."

Cara swallowed audibly. "So Susan's mother is—" She broke off. There was no need to finish the sentence out loud.

For a moment there was a stunned silence at the table as the noise of the cafeteria swirled around them. Then Lila glanced casually at her watch and gave a little gasp of dismay. "Oh, no! I'm going to be late. I'll see you later."

As Lila stood up, Cara grabbed her arm. "Are you sure about this?"

An unpleasant sensation of guilt washed over Lila for a brief moment, but she quickly pushed it out of her mind. "Well," she said slowly, "*nobody* really knows anything for sure, do they?"

Then she carefully removed Cara's hand from her arm and walked away. As she passed by Susan's table she felt a surge of triumph overcoming the guilt, and she strode out of the cafeteria with a victorious smile.

Six

On the following afternoon, Jessica opened the door of her room a crack and poked her head out. With a quick glance up and down the hall, she slipped out the door and closed it softly behind her.

Of course, she knew it was silly to worry about getting caught. After all, her parents were both at work, and Elizabeth knew what she was up to. But even though sneaking around was one of Jessica's specialties, she was always on the alert when she did. That was one of the reasons she almost never got caught in the act.

She tightened her grip on the bundle of clothes she was carrying—her excuse, if caught—and tiptoed silently down the hall to her parents' room.

Just as she put her hand on the door knob, a

quiet sound behind her caused her to freeze in her tracks. Breathlessly she waited for her fate to descend on her.

But after several seconds had passed with no bolt of lightning, she turned around slowly. Prince Albert was standing behind her, grinning his goofy, doggy grin at her.

Her breath exploded in a giggle. "Prince Albert, you moron! Are you trying to give me a heart attack?"

He wagged his tail happily and nuzzled her outstretched hand.

"OK," she said sternly, rubbing his silky gold ears. "You can help, but be *quiet*."

Immediately the dog assumed a serious and responsible expression, and Jessica couldn't help laughing at him. "Come on," she said chuckling softly, opening the door of her parents' bedroom.

Once they were both inside, she tossed the borrowed clothes onto the bed and stood in the middle of the room, hands on her hips, looking around her. She didn't know just what she was looking for, but if there was any evidence to be found that proved her mother was pregnant, she would find it.

For a moment, however, her attention was caught by the group of framed pictures arranged on her mother's dresser. She and her twin and their brother Steven were shown from infancy on up to the present. Jessica picked up a photograph of herself and Elizabeth dressed in identical pink-checkered pinafores at their third birthday party. She knew she was the one reaching a pudgy hand for the pile of presents.

"Look how little we were," she murmured, speaking more to herself than to the puppy. "And look at this one."

She picked up another photograph, which showed a much younger Ned Wakefield proudly holding up his first child, baby Steven.

Looking at the baby pictures suddenly filled Jessica with a profound feeling of excitement. As she brushed away an unexpected tear, she decided that if her mother was expecting a baby, she wanted to know. *Now*.

Prince Albert ambled over to the large walk-in closet and sniffed at the handle.

"You think that's the place to start looking, huh?" she said, whirling around, ready for action. "A maternity top—that's it!"

She was across the room to the closet in three long strides and yanked the door open. The orderly contents of her mother's closet faced her, daring her to disturb the neat organization.

With another quick listen for car doors or footsteps on the stairs, Jessica picked up a belt from the pile on the bed and held it loosely while she began her search. That way she could prove she was just returning it if someone turned up unexpectedly.

Making as little disturbance as possible, Jessica went through all the clothes that were in the closet. She unzipped garment bags and groped through stacked-up sweaters. After a few moments she began to think she might be on a wild-goose chase.

"Albert! What are you doing!" she cried suddenly as she noticed the retriever pawing at a pile of things in one corner.

She dropped to her knees, anxiously examining the objects in the heap for signs of damage. Prince Albert looked on expectantly. Behind an old pair of sandals, an outdated macramé handbag and a tattered beach blanket, Jessica's hand touched rustling paper. She drew out a paper bag eagerly.

The words "Great Expectations" marched cheerfully across the bag in pink-and-blue lettering, and a cluster of yellow balloons adorned one corner. It was from a downtown maternity and baby shop Jessica had seen.

With shaking hands, Jessica opened the bag and looked inside. She gasped, then crushed the bag. Prince Albert cocked his head as she met his gaze, and he began to pant softly.

Jessica swallowed and looked inside the bag again. Maybe she had just imagined the tiny yellow crocheted sweater and cap. No. She hadn't.

"Let's get out of here," she whispered hoarsely, stumbling to her feet. She stuffed the baby clothes back behind the pile of odds and ends and backed out of the closet.

"We've got to tell Liz," she continued, hastily shoving the rest of the borrowed clothes into a drawer. "Let's go."

She ran lightly to the door and, without even checking to see if all was clear, dashed down the hallway to her room. Now all she could do was wait for her sister to get home.

When Elizabeth opened the front door at six o'clock, she immediately sensed something in the air. She paused on the threshold, trying to figure out what it could be.

"What's wrong?" Jeffrey asked, narrowly avoiding walking into her as she stopped short.

"Oh, sorry," she replied quickly and stepped into the hall. "Do you believe in psychic powers?" she asked, arching her eyebrows provocatively.

The tall, blond-haired boy looked into her laughing, blue-green eyes for a moment without speaking. Then, with a lopsided grin, he snorted, "No, and neither do you!"

"That's what you think," Elizabeth continued as she shrugged out of her jacket. "But I can tell you right now, my sister is lurking around here somewhere, getting ready to pounce."

"Come on!" Jeffrey scoffed, his green eyes warm with laughter. "That's not psychic, that's just knowing Jessica."

"Just you wait! You'll see."

"Liz? Is that you?" a voice called from the kitchen.

"Yes, Mom!" Elizabeth turned to Jeffrey again. "Help me set the table, OK?"

"Anything for a psychic of your great powers, Madame Elizabeth."

"Ha-ha."

The two walked through the Wakefields' comfortable house to the kitchen. Mrs. Wakefield was sitting at the table, frowning over a cookbook, and Jessica was hovering near the kitchen door in a state of great agitation.

"Hi, Mom. Hi, Jess."

"Liz—Oh, hello, Jeffrey," Mrs. Wakefield said, running a hand through her short blond hair. "Liz, can you read what this says? There's a big blob of something right where it says how long to cook it for."

As Elizabeth moved to her mother's side, she noticed Jessica gesturing frantically from behind their mother's back. Her twin was widening her eyes and jerking her head toward the patio door in the adjoining dining room. Elizabeth paused for a moment, staring in amazement at her sister's bizarre pantomime and then turned to examine the illegible recipe.

"Looks like three-twenty-five for thirty minutes to me," she said, squinting at the open book. "But it could be three-seventy-five for ninety minutes. Hard to tell."

"Great!" Her mother groaned. "Either way, I stand an equal chance of disaster. It could turn out either burned or raw. Well, I'll just make a fritatta, I guess. Jessica, what on *earth* are you doing?" she added, turning around and catching a glimpse of her younger daughter's antics.

Jessica's face instantly became a blank, and she slouched against a cupboard in an attitude of studied nonchalance. "Nothing," she replied in a surprised voice. "Just standing here." Her eyes were wide with innocence.

"Well, you looked as if you were having some kind of a fit."

Elizabeth pressed her lips together to keep from laughing while Jessica looked sheepish. She sent Jeffrey an I-told-you-so wink and got a wry smile in return.

"Liz, would you please take over here," her mother said, pushing herself up from the table. "Just use these vegetables, and there are plenty of eggs, for the fritatta, OK? And, Jeffrey, I've got some big boxes in my car that I would *love* for you to help me with."

"Sure," he replied quickly, holding the door open.

Jessica watched as they left the kitchen, and

as soon as the door swung shut, she swooped down on her twin.

"Liz!" she hissed, grabbing her arm. "You'll never believe it!"

Elizabeth couldn't help laughing as she took eggs from the refrigerator to make the Italian-style omelette. Then she remembered the raid her sister had planned for that afternoon. "Well?" she asked, suddenly taking Jessica's feverish impatience more seriously.

With a quick glance at the door, Jessica whispered, "I found some brand-new baby clothes."

For a moment, Elizabeth stared at her twin without comprehending what she had heard. Her face felt as though it were stuck in one blank, stupid expression. Until then, she hadn't quite believed Jessica's theory. But now . . . Finally she cleared her throat. "What did you say?"

Jessica joined her at the counter, and began breaking the eggs in a bowl, then added some milk. "I found a baby sweater and a little hat type of thing—a baby bonnet—in Mom's closet." She feverishly beat the mixture.

There was another tense pause. Elizabeth's knife was poised motionless over the onions and peppers she was chopping.

"Then she really—"

"Yes."

The twins looked solemnly at each other for a

moment. Then Elizabeth continued chopping. "But I don't understand why she won't—"

"Maybe she thinks we'd be upset or something," Jessica interrupted. She took some cheese out of the refrigerator and began grating it. "Maybe she just . . ." Her voice trailed off.

But Elizabeth shook her head decisively. "Jess, it's silly of us to pretend we don't know. Let's just go ask Mom if it's true." She put the chopped vegetables into the egg mixture.

"You think we should?" Jessica regarded Elizabeth skeptically.

"I—"

Jeffrey strode into the kitchen and stopped short when he saw the girls' serious, intent faces. "You want me to . . . ?" He gestured at the door behind him.

"Yes—no, I mean . . ." Elizabeth frowned in concentration. "Could you just finish this up, Jeff? Just add the cheese, stir everything together, and then pour it into this pan." She put a large frying pan on the burner and added margarine. "Let it cook on low heat. We'll be back in a few minutes."

He shrugged. "Sure. Anything wrong?"

But the girls didn't stop to answer. With nervous anticipation they rushed out of the kitchen, looking for their mother. Outside their father's den they heard voices.

"Dad's home," Jessica whispered, nodding toward the closed door.

"Good. We can talk to both of them." But as Elizabeth reached for the knob, Mrs. Wakefield's voice came through distinctly.

"I don't know, Ned. I'd rather not tell them until we're sure. I don't know how they'll take it."

"Come on, sweetheart. They're old enough to handle the responsibility."

"I know, I know. But I just don't know how to break it to them, that's all. Let's just wait until it's definite, OK?"

Elizabeth and Jessica stared at each other, stunned. Then they tiptoed into the living room.

"She thinks we'll freak out or something," Jessica whispered. "She doesn't want to tell us."

Elizabeth frowned. "I know. We should really respect her decision to wait before she tells us, though. But how can we let her know we aren't upset?"

"I know! Our plan about dropping hints," Jessica suggested, brightening. "We can start at dinner to let them know how happy we'd be. You know."

Nodding earnestly, Elizabeth opened her mouth to speak, but the study door opened, and they both jumped guiltily. A moment later their father walked into the living room. "Hi, Daddy," Elizabeth said, hoping she sounded calm.

Ned Wakefield was loosening his tie. "Hi, princess. And, hi, princess, to you, too," he added, touching Jessica's cheek lightly.

"What's this powwow about?" Mrs. Wakefield asked, joining them in the living room. "You both look like you're plotting some evil conspiracy."

"Oh, we were just talking, Mom," Jessica began, throwing her twin a quick look. "We were talking about, you know, kids."

Their mother nodded. "Oh."

"Yeah, kids. Having kids. Liz said she wants to have a lot of kids."

Elizabeth jumped, but she quickly recovered and nodded emphatically. "That's right. I love big families. Lots of kids."

"Well that's nice, Liz. Is dinner ready yet?"

With a twinge of guilt, Elizabeth admitted, "Actually, I left Jeffrey in charge. And I still have to make the salad."

"Well, let's go rescue him," Mr. Wakefield said with a chuckle. "He's probably in a state of near panic by now."

The Wakefields and Jeffrey were sitting at the table eating the fritatta, salad, and crusty Italian bread when Elizabeth took a deep breath and said casually, "I always wished we had more

73

brothers and sisters." She looked studiously at her plate as she picked at her salad.

"Me, too," Jessica chimed in. "I always used to pretend my dolls were my baby brothers and sisters and I had to take care of them. But I was glad to do it," she added with an anxious glance at her mother.

Elizabeth saw Jeffrey staring at her twin in surprise. It did sound sort of dumb, she realized.

Mrs. Wakefield put down her fork carefully and looked at Jessica. "I never knew that, Jess."

"Oh, sure. All I ever wanted was to have a baby to take care of," she insisted, looking at both her parents.

"Yeah. And I always thought it would be fun to have someone younger to give advice to and help with homework and stuff," added Elizabeth.

Across the table, Mr. and Mrs. Wakefield exchanged a look of surprise, and Elizabeth's heart leaped. Her parents hadn't realized how glad she and Jessica would be if their mother was pregnant. Maybe now they'd feel ready to admit it was true.

"I just love babies," she continued pointedly.

Her father wiped his mouth with his napkin and gave Jeffrey a wry smile. "Listen, Jeff. I think it's time you reconsidered your association with this family. Obviously Liz is cracking up."

Elizabeth blushed, and she gave her twin a pleading look.

"Liz isn't crazy, Dad. It's just that well—" Jessica paused, biting her lip. "A friend of ours at school's mother had a baby, and we thought that must be fantastic for her. You know, to have a baby in the house."

Their mother nodded. "I see." She glanced at her husband, a slightly worried frown on her face.

An awkward silence descended over the table for a few moments. Then Mrs. Wakefield said abruptly, "Girls, I'd like to talk to you both after dinner, all right?"

Elizabeth's eyes met Jessica's across the table, and she gave her twin an excited grin. "Sure, Mom."

"Yeah, Mom. Sure."

It worked! She's going to tell us! Elizabeth told herself exultantly. *She's going to tell us she's having a baby!*

Seven

Jessica stared morosely out the kitchen window at the glint of sunlight sparkling on the swimming pool. Even a typically brilliant Sweet Valley morning wasn't enough to lift her spirits. Her mind replayed the previous night's humiliating scene, and she gave an inward groan.

Across the table, she noticed Elizabeth stirring her coffee in a desultory way. Jessica shuddered, and Elizabeth looked up.

"Pretty embarrassing, huh?"

With a heavy sigh, Jessica shook her head. "Honestly. When Mom looked at us and said, 'Which one of you is in trouble?' I nearly died."

"Yeah. I guess we kind of overdid it about saying how much we wanted to have a baby." Elizabeth's shoulders sagged. "But I don't know

77

what else we can do," she complained. "She still won't admit she's pregnant."

"We'll just have to keep it up. I mean, now that she knows we're not talking about *us*, it's got to be pretty obvious we're talking about her."

"Good morning!" Alice Wakefield came into the kitchen, a beaming smile on her face. "Did anyone get the newspaper—oh, there it is." She rested her hand on Elizabeth's shoulder briefly as she sat down and reached for the *Sweet Valley News*.

Jessica rolled her eyes and finished off her orange juice.

"Hmm," said her mother, pouring coffee into her favorite mug. "It says there that Jackson Croft, that famous movie director, is coming to Sweet Valley to make a film."

In an instant, Jessica's frustration evaporated. Her eyes lit up, and she asked, "Coming here?"

"Yes. And, girls! Listen to this: 'Next Saturday he will be holding an open casting call for extras at the Hampton Place shopping center parking lot.' That sounds like a lot of fun, doesn't it?"

Visions of Jessica Wakefield, glamorous movie star, flashed through Jessica's head. Being a movie extra seemed like the logical first step to superstardom. She could see it now: She'd start out in light, romantic comedy films and then move on to the heavy, powerful dramas that Croft was so famous for.

And it wasn't as though she were completely inexperienced either, she reminded herself with some satisfaction. She'd had the lead in the school production of *Splendor in the Grass*, she had been on Jeremy Frank's talk show on TV, and she'd been in a modeling show at the Valley Mall. That would definitely impress Jackson Croft, she thought.

She noticed the twinkle in her sister's eye as Elizabeth looked across the table at her. "What are you looking at?" Jessica asked, knowing full well that Elizabeth had just read her mind.

"Oh, nothing. Think you'll go to this casting call?"

Jessica stuck her tongue out at her twin. "Maybe. Well sure, why not?" she continued defensively as her mother started grinning, too.

With a light laugh, Mrs. Wakefield shook her head. "Oh, Jess, you're so transparent. You think you'll be in Hollywood by the end of the month, don't you?"

"All she has to do is hear 'movie director,' and she starts plotting," Elizabeth added with a wicked grin.

"I am *not* plotting," Jessica said haughtily. "I just happen to think it would be very *interesting* to go to a casting call, that's all."

Elizabeth nodded solemnly. "Oh, right."

"And besides, Jackson Croft is a very famous and respected film director. I'd be honored just to see him."

With a thoughtful smile, Elizabeth leaned over her mother's shoulder to read the article. "That's true," she agreed, looking over the list of his movies. "I can't think of any other director who combines entertainment with a real message."

" 'A critical and popular success,' " her mother read out loud. " 'Jackson Croft's unerring sense of the issues that capture the public's heart has made him one of the foremost directors in the business. He has been honored at Cannes and by the Motion Picture Academy and has received numerous humanitarian awards.' Talk about having your cake and eating it too," she added with a dry smile.

"Does it say what movie he's coming here to do?" Jessica asked.

Mrs. Wakefield shook her head. "No—oh, wait. Here it is. It's called *La Luna*. All it says is that it's a drama about one year in the life of a family. That's all it says, though."

"He'd get plenty of drama out of our family in one year, that's for sure." Elizabeth chuckled. "With Jessica around, life is never dull."

But Jessica didn't even hear her sister teasing her. She couldn't wait to tell Lila and Cara about Jackson Croft and the casting call. That was even better than the news about Susan

Stewart, as far as she was concerned. After all, now that Susan was a nobody, who cared about her? But getting into the movies—now *that* was something to talk about.

"Susan! It's for you!"

"OK, Aunt Helen. I'll be right there." Susan finished washing her hands and glanced at her watch. Who would be calling so early in the morning? She ran lightly down the hallway and picked up the phone.

"Hello?"

"Susan, this is Deborah Carteret."

"Hi, Deborah! How are you? Are we all set for tonight?" The girl was one of Susan's wealthy Bridgewater friends, and she had invited Susan over for dinner that evening.

Deborah's voice held a note of constraint as she replied, "Well, actually, that's why I'm calling. Something has suddenly come up, Susan. I'm afraid I'll have to cancel the dinner invite."

"Oh. Nothing serious, I hope," Susan said, hoping her disappointment wasn't too obvious.

"Actually, it is. Quite serious."

"Oh, Deborah, I'm sorry to hear that."

"Yes," the girl said distantly. "So am I. Goodbye."

Susan stared at the phone: it had gone dead in her hand before she could say anything else.

Deborah had sounded so strange, as though she were angry at her, Susan thought. She fought back the vague feeling of uneasiness that had been haunting her for two days. Everywhere she went, she felt she was being watched and talked about—in an unmistakably negative way.

It had started the other afternoon. At first she thought it was just her imagination: it was just a coincidence that conversations came to a halt when she appeared. But the day before, there had been no way to ignore it. People were definitely avoiding her. Even Gordon. And now Deborah Carteret had canceled their dinner date.

"Everything OK, Susan?"

She jumped, startled out of her reverie. "Oh, sure. Sure, Aunt Helen. And I'll be home for dinner after all," she added as brightly as she could.

A look of concern flashed across Mrs. Reister's face. "What about going to Bridgewater?"

"Oh, something came up suddenly, and Deborah said she had to postpone it." *Although she didn't say anything about rescheduling*, Susan realized.

"That's too bad."

"Hmm," Susan murmured, avoiding her guardian's eyes. She toyed absently with the phone cord for a moment, unaware that Mrs. Reister was looking at her intently. "Well, I'd better get to school, I guess."

"If you get home right after school, we could go look for some dress material this afternoon. How would that be?"

Susan nodded. "Sure." With a feeling of dread she picked up her book bag, but she managed a weak smile. " 'Bye." She opened the door and walked out of the house.

It was a short walk to school, but as she drew nearer to the school, she walked more slowly. When she reached the school, she stopped to look up at the columned facade and ornate Romanesque clock. Never in her life had she been unsure of her welcome: she had always been well received wherever she went. But for the first time, she was nervous about seeing the people she knew. She drew a deep breath, then walked across the lawn and up the front steps.

A group of boys sitting halfway up stopped talking and turned to look at Susan with expressionless faces. A cold shiver ran up her spine, but she kept walking. *What is going on?* she wanted to scream. *Why is everyone looking at me that way?*

Every single person she passed managed to avoid eye contact with her, and she had a horrible sensation of being invisible. But she was sure that as soon as she had passed, people were staring at her without any difficulty. She opened her locker with fumbling, clumsy fingers and blindly grabbed her morning books.

She walked into each class as though going to her own execution. Whenever she dared to speak to anyone, she was answered in monosyllables. Between her classes she kept looking for Gordon, wishing she had his reassuring strength to comfort her, but he was nowhere to be found. By the end of the day she felt as if she were living in a nightmare, and she hardly raised her eyes at all as she walked stiffly down the hallway.

She stopped at her locker and racked her brain trying to think of what books she needed. But her mind was a blank. She heard a cough behind her but didn't pay any attention to the sound.

There was another cough, and then the sound of Gordon's voice. "Uh, Susan?"

She whirled around. "Oh! Oh, Gordon, am I glad to see you!" she said, smiling in relief. "I've been looking all over for you. Where've you been?"

He smiled thinly. "Oh, I don't know," he mumbled. "Around, I guess."

Feeling she could relax at last, Susan leaned back against the lockers and breathed deeply. "What a day. I must be cracking up. I swear people were staring at me everywhere I went."

Gordon looked quickly over his shoulder, and his eyes met hers briefly again. Then he looked at the floor and said nothing.

"But I've decided I'm just going to ignore it,"

Susan continued, oblivious of Gordon's peculiar manner. "I'm going to buy the material for my ball dress this afternoon. Tell your mom I'm taking her advice. It's going to be gold."

A dull red blush washed over Gordon's handsome features, and he coughed into his fist. It was a dry, forced kind of cough. Susan began to feel alarmed.

"Well, ummm, about the Bridgewater Ball," he said, avoiding her eyes, "I have to—I can't . . ."

Now Susan's throat felt dry, too, and the nightmarish quality came flooding back. "What are you trying to tell me, Gordon?"

"I—" He closed his mouth with a snap, then burst out, "I can't take you to the ball."

She stared at him speechless. After what she had been through that day, she hardly felt any surprise at all. But it didn't make any sense! "Why?" she whispered finally.

"Well, my parents—they, uh, they don't think I should take you."

"Your parents? Your parents?" she repeated mechanically. But the Stoddards liked her, didn't they?

Gordon shifted his feet uncomfortably and said nothing.

"Your parents don't want you to take me. But what about you?" Confusion was stronger than pain at the moment: She just didn't understand why this was happening. "Don't you still like me?"

"I—you know I—my parents—" Gordon gestured futilely.

"But, Gordon, I don't get it! You're doing this because your parents told you to? Why?"

He looked around quickly as she raised her voice, and the color deepened in his cheeks. "Susan," he began, his voice shaking with suppressed emotion. "Susan, you know what people are saying."

The loud pounding in her ears was her heartbeat, Susan realized through a fog. "No, I *don't* know what people are saying. What *are* they saying?" she asked, her voice coming from far away.

Gordon suddenly exploded with indignant anger. "You know perfectly well, Susan, so you can cut out the big innocent act! Your mother killed someone, and she's been locked up your whole life in an asylum!"

She said nothing. She couldn't speak.

"Why did you have to lie, Susan? What gave you the right to tell everyone you were so important?" Gordon stared at her furiously for another few moments. Then he spun around on his heel and walked away.

Susan felt as if the world were whirling around her, as if she were drowning in a sea of confusion. She felt hot, and then cold, and scorching

tears began streaming down her cheeks. With a
strangled cry, she ran down the hall away from
the direction Gordon had gone. She didn't know
where she was going and barely realized where
she was when she stumbled around the corner
of the echoing, deserted corridor and slammed
into someone.

"What the—! Susan!" Allen Walters stared at
her, catching her in a strong grip. He took one
look at her and steered her into an empty classroom, kicking the door shut behind them.

Suddenly Susan found herself sobbing in his
arms, crying as though her heart would break.
Allen awkwardly patted her back and made
soft, soothing sounds into her hair.

"Shh, shh. Susan, it's OK. Don't cry," he
whispered, holding her gently. "Don't worry,
it's OK."

"You don't understand!" she said in a choked
voice, as she leaned into his chest. "You don't
understand!"

"I understand," he murmured. "Don't talk,
just try to relax. It's OK."

Finally, the painful, wrenching sobs quieted.
Susan lifted her head, sniffing. "I'm—I'm sorry,"
she said, seeing Allen as though for the first
time. She looked around her in confusion and
sat slowly on the edge of a desk. "I hope I
didn't make you miss your bus or something."

He waved his hand impatiently. "Forget it. I

drove to school." He looked gravely into her eyes. "Do you want to tell me what's wrong? I mean, I'm not very good at advice or anything. But I'm a good listener."

She pressed her palm against her trembling chin and met his serious gaze. The sympathy and warmth she saw there gave her the strength to speak. "I guess you haven't heard, huh?"

"I have, but I don't believe it," he said angrily. "Don't tell me you do?"

Another sob threatened to surface, and she forced herself to control it. "I don't know! I don't know what to believe. I don't even know how everybody knew about it except me."

"Listen," Allen said. "It doesn't make sense just to accept something like that without question. Find out if it's true; that's what I think you should do."

Susan looked bleakly up into the tall boy's face. "What if it *is* true?" she whispered.

But he shook his head, then put his hands on her shoulders. "It isn't. But even if it were, do you think it would make any difference to me?"

She couldn't answer.

"Look, how about I drive you home, and you can ask your— Is she your aunt?"

"My guardian." She sighed, lowering her head. She looked up again and found strength in his serious, intense eyes. "OK." She nodded and squared her shoulders. "I'll ask Aunt Helen."

*　*　*

Susan stood on the sidewalk, watching as Allen Walters drove away. Then she walked up the steps to her front door and entered the house.

"Susan! You're late. I'm not sure we'll have time to go—" Mrs. Reister looked into the hall from the kitchen, a rueful smile on her face. But the sight of Susan's face froze the words on her lips.

"Susan, what is it? What's wrong?"

Holding herself very straight, Susan walked into the small living room and faced out the window. Her voice was low as she said, "Aunt Helen, I have to know who my mother is. I think I'll die if you don't tell me," she added, her heart full of pain.

She watched the leaves of the trees rustling in a slight breeze. But she felt very far removed, as though much more than a thin pane of glass separated her from the rest of the world. The silence in the room was overwhelming.

Finally she turned around. Mrs. Reister was staring at her speechlessly, her face a picture of anguish.

Susan's heart began to pound. *"Who is my mother?"* she begged. "Please! Please, Aunt Helen! Tell me! I have to know!"

"I—can't—tell you," the woman said, forcing the words out one by one. She met Susan's eyes, her own pain obvious. "Susan, I can't tell you." Drawing a shaky breath, Mrs. Reister added, "I have to go to work now. I'll see you later."

Susan closed her eyes. *Then it's true!* a voice inside her screamed. *It's true! It's true!* When she opened her eyes again, Mrs. Reister was gone. Susan's knees buckled under her, and she collapsed onto the sofa, crying bitterly.

Eight

Elizabeth stared absentmindedly at the contents of the refrigerator. Nothing looked absolutely irresistible, and she realized she wasn't really hungry anyway. She poured herself a glass of root beer and sat down at the kitchen table.

Lying next to her was the morning paper, and she picked it up, glad for a free moment to read. Her eye caught the headline "World-Renowned Director Comes to Sweet Valley," and she grinned, thinking about Jessica's optimistic scheming. Her twin was absolutely convinced she was destined for superstardom.

But her smile faded when she read the subhead, "Tragic Death of Son." Taking a slow swallow of root beer, she read the rest of the article.

This will be the first project Croft has taken on since the car accident last year

91

that claimed the life of his only child, fourteen-year-old Jason Croft. Croft and his wife, actress Veronica Hammond, were also in the accident but escaped serious injury. The crash was blamed on a drunk driver.

Croft and his wife were both said to be devastated by their loss and have refused to appear in public until recently. Ms. Hammond is said to have turned down several movie parts. Croft is now proceding with his new film, *La Luna*, only after "serious consideration and soul searching." "Jason loved to help out on my movies," the director said in a recently released statement. "*La Luna* will be dedicated to his memory." The director's earnings for the film will be donated to SADD, Students Against Drunk Driving, according to Croft's agent.

Elizabeth lowered the newspaper and looked off into space. "How could you go on after something like that?" she wondered aloud.

Elizabeth sighed deeply. Jackson Croft must be a pretty special person, she decided, especially if he was donating his profits to SADD. An idea formed in her head as she sat gazing at the open newspaper. Maybe . . .

She sat up straighter, biting her lower lip, and stared intently at a hanging ivy plant without seeing it. Maybe she could interview him for *The Oracle,* she thought with growing excitement. *He has a real message about drunk driving, and kids really respect him,* she thought. *I bet he'd give a school reporter a chance to talk to him!*

The more she thought about it, the more convinced Elizabeth became that she could—and should—get an interview with Jackson Croft. But how to get to him? A famous director was probably surrounded by a dozen secretaries, assistants, and PR people. If only there was some way to get to him when he was out in public.

Elizabeth sat bolt upright and snatched up the paper again. The casting call! Of course! He'd be there, talking to all kinds of people. She could go and introduce herself and ask if she could interview him at a later time! This could be her biggest story ever. Louis Westman, the school editor at the *Sweet Valley News,* might even reprint it.

Lost in her own daydream of success, Elizabeth was barely aware of the screeching of tires on the street outside. But when the front door slammed and feet pounded down the hall, she came to pretty quickly.

"Liz! What's wrong? Who's hurt? What happened?"

Steven Wakefield, the twins' eighteen-year-old brother, stood staring at her, his chest heaving and his dark eyes wide with alarm.

"Steve! What are you talking about?" Elizabeth said, her mouth dropping open with surprise.

He threw himself into a chair beside her and clasped her hand. "Listen, whatever it is, we can pull through together. Don't hold back on me, Liz."

"But, Steve, I don't know what you're talking about. Honest!"

Puzzled, he stared at her. Elizabeth was once again struck by the strong resemblance her dark and handsome brother bore to their father. Digging into his pocket, he pulled out a crumpled sheet of paper and flung it on the table. "Well, what's this all about, then?"

Scribbled on the paper was a message: "Steve— your sister called and said there's a family emergency. Get home right away, no time to lose."

"That was on my door when I got back to the dorm after class," Elizabeth's brother explained, tapping the note with one forefinger. "So what's the big family emergency?"

Obviously the message was Jessica's handiwork, but what it meant was a mystery. Unless—

Elizabeth shook her head. "Well, I wouldn't exactly call it an emergency, but it is really important, so I'm glad you're here."

"Well?" he demanded impatiently. "What is it?"

"I don't know how to say this except to say—"

"*Steve!* You're here."

Jessica raced across the room and grabbed her brother in a grateful hug. When she had extricated herself, she turned to Elizabeth. "What does he think we should do about it?"

"Do about what? Will one of you *please* tell me what is going on here?"

Jessica's eyes widened, and she pointed an accusing finger at her twin. "Didn't you tell him, Liz?"

"Tell me *what*?" Steven roared, getting to his feet in angry frustration.

Both girls stared at him in surprise. "That Mom's pregnant," Jessica said flatly.

For a moment Steven's mouth hung open, and then he closed it slowly and sank back into his chair. "Would you say that again?" he asked faintly.

Elizabeth laughed. "Oh, Steve! You look so funny!"

"This is no laughing matter," Jessica cut in tersely. She took a seat across from her brother and explained everything they had discovered and pieced together about their mother's condition, and about her apparent reluctance to tell them about it.

"So we're trying to let them know how happy we'd be if they'd just come out and tell us," she concluded, crossing her arms and fixing Steven with a stern, businesslike look.

He looked back at her blankly.

"Well? Come on, Steve. Say something."

Suddenly a huge grin broke over his handsome face, and he burst out laughing. "OK, OK, Jess! You really had me going there. That's a good one, though." He chuckled and punched her lightly on the arm. "Mom's pregnant! Right!"

The twins stared at him, speechless. After a moment Elizabeth gasped, "But, Steve, it's no joke. Honest."

He looked from Elizabeth to Jessica and back again, the grin fading away. "No joke?"

Shaking her head solemnly, Elizabeth repeated, "No joke."

They gave him a few minutes to let the news sink in completely.

"Whew." He sighed. Then he nodded decisively. "I guess the only thing is to keep up the 'we love babies' campaign."

Jessica nodded eagerly. "That's what I thought. And now that you'll be doing it, too, why should they wait any longer, right?"

"Right. You know, I—"

The kitchen door swung open, and Mrs. Wakefield staggered in with two armloads of grocery bags. "Steve! I saw your car outside and—"

"Mom! Give me those bags!" Steven yelled, springing to his feet with a look of horror.

Mrs. Wakefield looked on in amazement as her son grabbed the groceries and dumped them unceremoniously on the counter. "Here," he continued, pulling her toward a chair. "Sit down. Don't tire yourself out like that!"

All she could do was stare at him. Finally she opened her mouth. "Hello, Steve. What are you doing home from college?" she said evenly.

"I just wanted to see you, Mom. How are you feeling? Can I get you anything?"

Elizabeth tried to get his attention. He was being much too obvious, she thought.

Mrs. Wakefield's look of astonishment grew even more pronounced. "How am I *feeling*?"

"Let me take your jacket. Do you want Liz to make you some tea or something?"

Mrs. Wakefield surrendered her jacket with trancelike calm, and he hung it on the back of a chair. Finally she turned her eyes to Elizabeth. "What's with *him*?" she mouthed, her blue eyes wide with amazement.

Elizabeth darted a quick look at Jessica, hoping to find some inspiration. But Jessica looked just as blank as she did, and she ducked out of the situation by jumping up to put away groceries.

"Umm." Elizabeth's mind raced as she tried to find a good way to explain Steven's bizarre behavior. "Uh, Steve just wanted to come home and spend some time with the family," she explained weakly. "He loves family life." She gulped, then turned to Steven for help.

"Yeah," he put in hastily. "That's right. There's nothing like being with your own family."

His mother eyed him suspiciously. She looked as if she were about to say something but then changed her mind. With a puzzled shrug she announced, "I'm going upstairs to change my clothes. When I come down again, I hope my real children will have returned."

With that she got up from the table and went out of the room, leaving the three Wakefield children to stare at one another gloomily.

Steven knocked gently on the study door. "Dad, got a minute?"

Putting down his papers, Mr. Wakefield called, "Of course, Steve. Come in."

When he had closed the door carefully behind him, Steven stood awkwardly, ill at ease and suddenly embarrassed.

His father gave him a questioning look. "Something on your mind, son?"

"Well, Dad, what I—"

"Sit down, Steve."

Steven nodded impatiently and sat on the edge of a chair. With what he hoped was a mature, responsible expression, he started again. "Dad, I've been thinking, and I just wanted you to know that if Mom—well, if she ever had to quit working—for—some reason . . ." His voice trailed off, his cheeks burning.

Mr. Wakefield folded his arms and surveyed his son thoughtfully. "Yes?"

"Well—" Steven stretched his throat and scratched the back of his neck, avoiding his father's steady gaze. "Well, I just wanted to let you know I'd be willing to quit school and get a job to help out. That's all," he finished in a rush.

Slowly and with meticulous care, Mr. Wakefield lined up a handful of paper clips on his desk blotter. He nodded. "I see. And may I ask what brought this up?"

Steven looked away from his father, afraid he might give the whole show away. "I just wanted you to know you can count on me, Dad. I'm willing to pull my share of the load around here to help our family."

"Well, Steve, I must say I'm a little puzzled—not that I don't really appreciate your generous offer," he added quickly. "But I think we can manage without your giving up your education." His face was grave as he said, "We'll squeak by somehow."

Suddenly Steven was overcome, and he strode across the room to his father. "Oh, Dad!" he exclaimed, hugging his father tightly, his voice quavering with emotion. Then he turned and ran out of the study, leaving Mr. Wakefield staring after him in astonishment.

*　　*　　*

Jessica frantically tossed clothes aside as she searched for the telephone. Another ring and whoever was calling would give up. With a triumphant cry she unearthed the phone and grabbed up the receiver. "Hello?" she said breathlessly.

"Jess? Is that you?"

Throwing herself on her bed, Jessica cradled the phone on her shoulder. "Hi, Lila. What's up?"

"Wellll . . . something really unbelievable has happened."

Jessica rolled her eyes. Apparently Lila was in her drag-it-out-as-long-as-possible mood. "Yeah?" she drawled, leafing through the pages of a recent issue of *Glamour*. "Unbelievably good or unbelievably bad?"

"Well . . . bad. I never realized before what a total jerk Gordon Stoddard is. I mean, how could he do it?"

This is going to take all night, Jessica thought. "OK, what did he do?"

"Well, I was at the club with Daddy having dinner—we do that when he's in town, you know."

I know, I know. "What did *Gordon* do?"

"The Stoddards were there—not Gordon, though, the jerk—and they said they'd never been so shocked in their whole lives as when they heard about Susan Stewart." Lila paused for dramatic effect.

Jessica sat up a little more attentively. "And?" she prompted.

"And they said wasn't she awful to try to trap Gordon into a relationship, and they had told him to stop seeing her, and he broke their date for the Bridgewater Ball!"

"*No!* You're kidding!" Jessica was now sitting completely upright on her bed, the magazine forgotten. Her mind worked quickly, reading between the lines of Lila's story. "Hmm, maybe he'll ask you, then," she said finally.

"Oh, I'd never go anywhere with someone so shallow," Lila replied hastily. But her voice wasn't entirely convincing. "I mean, just because there's a *rumor* that Susan's, well . . ."

"Yeah, yeah. But seriously, Lila. Are you saying you wouldn't go to the Bridgewater Ball with Gordon if he asked you to?"

"I wouldn't go to the end of the street with him if it were up to me," Lila retorted haughtily. "But you know what social obligations are. I might have to go for my father's sake, even though, to tell you the truth, I think the whole idea is sickening. But the Fowlers and the Stoddards have always been friends."

For a moment Jessica squinted suspiciously at the phone in her hand. That was laying it on a little thick, wasn't it? Lila made it sound as though the Fowlers had been millionaire socialites for years instead of being "new money."

"So you would go if Gordon asked you, in other words," Jessica said slowly.

"Well, you know how it is—"

"Yeah, no one else might ask," Jessica cut in sharply.

"That's not true!"

Jessica smiled sweetly. "Oh, of course not. Sorry, Lila."

There was an angry pause at the other end of the line. At last Lila said, "All I'm saying is, I'm not going out of my way to get him to ask me, but—"

"Yeah, I know. Social obligations and everything."

"Well, I've got to go, Jess. See you tomorrow."

"OK, 'bye, Lila," Jessica answered breezily. But as she hung up the phone, Jessica was thoughtful. So Gordon Stoddard needed a date for the Bridgewater Ball? And Lila wasn't going to go out of her way to get asked?

Well, I know someone who looks great in a floor-length ball dress, Jessica thought to herself with a slow, sly grin. *And it isn't Lila Fowler!*

Nine

"Hi, Liz."

"Hi, Jess." Elizabeth looked into the mirror at her twin, who was standing nonchalantly just inside the door in a lacy slip. "Something I can do for you?"

Jessica feigned surprise. "Gee, thanks, Liz! It's nice of you to ask. I do need to borrow something to wear," she said ingenuously. "Every single thing I own is totally wrinkled."

The merest glimmer of annoyance passed over Elizabeth's face. Sharing clothes with Jessica was always a one-way street. But on the other hand, she told herself as she fastened a pair of tiny gold heart earrings in her ears, what else were sisters for? Besides, if she put up a fight, Jessica would find a way to win somehow. She always did.

"OK." She shrugged, turning to face her twin. "Did you have something in particular picked out already? As if I had to ask."

"Well, if you don't mind, I thought that blue dress that Heather made for you?" Jessica finished in a supplicating, hopeful tone and gave her sister her most winning smile.

"Jessica!" Elizabeth glared at her twin in frustration. Of all her dresses, why did Jessica have to pick that one? Her friend Heather Sanford, a self-taught fashion designer, had created the dress especially for her as a gift. Of light blue, feather-light cambric, it fit her size-six figure perfectly. She shook her head doubtfully. "Jess, Heather designed it just for me."

"Well, that's practically the same as designing it for me, too, right? I mean, we only have exactly the same body, you know."

Elizabeth felt herself wavering. "But isn't it a little conservative for you?" she asked, knowing full well that she was fighting a losing battle.

"Oh, I feel like looking conservative today, I guess." Jessica grinned and opened Elizabeth's closet. As she pulled out the demure but elegant dress, she added, "And you're the best sister in the whole world. I'll love you until the end of time!"

In spite of herself, Elizabeth grinned back. "OK, OK, you can wear it. I'm just a pushover, I guess. But how come the sudden plunge into the traditional look, Jess? Someone in particular you're trying to impress?"

"Well, actually . . ." came the muffled response as Jessica pulled the dress on over her head. She emerged through the top and began to struggle with the tiny pearl buttons that ran up the back. "Could you do these, Liz? Actually, I thought I'd try to get to know Gordon Stoddard a little better. He seems like a really—interesting guy."

Elizabeth's hands stopped on the buttons. "Gordon Stoddard? But he's Susan Stewart's boyfriend, Jessica."

"Not anymore. He dumped her when he found out that her mother is a lunatic. Susan probably is, too."

Shocked, Elizabeth stared at her twin's reflection. "But that's just a rumor! And even if it is true about her mother, that has nothing to do with Susan herself!"

"You'd better believe it does!" Jessica snorted. She turned around and faced Elizabeth. "After what that girl pulled about being someone important, she'll be lucky if anyone ever speaks to her again!"

Jessica tossed her head and flounced out of the room, and Elizabeth sat down on the edge of her bed. She had heard the rumor, of course. Everyone had. But she had no idea people would really be taking such a ludicrous story seriously.

And how could Gordon Stoddard be such a snob as to break up with Susan because of it?

Susan must be going out of her mind, Elizabeth thought with compassion. Nobody deserved to be treated that way!

"Lila! I've been looking everywhere for you! Oh, hello, Gordon," Jessica added sweetly as she sat down next to him at the lunch table.

"Hi—Jessica?" he replied dubiously, eyeing her modest, ladylike dress with some confusion. His handsome features were set in an expression of polite but uncertain attention.

She gave him a tinkling, lighthearted laugh and wagged a finger at him. "Gordon, don't you know me by now?" She smiled serenely at Lila, who was sending her a malevolent glare.

"Jessica, Gordon and I were in the middle of a pretty personal discussion," Lila said through clenched teeth. "So if you don't *mind*—"

"Oh, really? That's nice. Gordon, I wanted to ask you something," Jessica continued, turning away from Lila. "I'm planning to buy a new tennis racket, but I don't know if I should move up to a midsize or stick with the regular. What do you think I should do? I know you're a great tennis player—among other things," she added coyly. She opened her lustrous eyes wide as she smiled at him and tingled with delight when he smiled in return. Flattery had never let her down yet.

"Well, Jess—"

Lila reached across the table and put a hand on his arm. "Gordon, you said I could borrow your history notes, remember? And I have to go—somewhere—so could we get them now?"

Confused, Gordon looked from Lila to Jessica and then back to Lila again.

Jessica made a sour face. "Where do you have to go, Lila? Another one of your many *social obligations*?" she stressed, narrowing her eyes at her friend.

"That's right," Lila responded with mock cordiality. "Let's go, Gordon." With a brilliant smile, Lila steered Gordon away from the table and out of the cafeteria.

"You think you're so smart," Jessica muttered grumpily as she slouched down in her chair. "At this rate I'll be too busy baby-sitting for my new brother or sister to date anyone."

Elizabeth looked anxiously into the cafeteria, searching for Susan. But the girl was nowhere to be seen. Just as she turned away, she caught a glimpse of her twin, the delicate blue dress hiked up in back as Jessica slouched in a chair. *She's going to iron that or I'll kill her*, Elizabeth vowed silently, then hurried away down the hall.

Turning a corner, she ran into Bill Chase and DeeDee Gordon. "Liz!" DeeDee exclaimed with a smile. "Help me convince this dope to go to Jackson Croft's casting call."

Bill Chase was an aspiring actor, and DeeDee's father, a talent agent, had been working with him lately. But apparently Bill was having a sudden attack of stage fright.

"You really should, Bill," Elizabeth said quickly. "It's a good chance for you."

"Well, I guess I will. I don't know."

"Listen, have either of you guys seen Susan Stewart anywhere?" Elizabeth continued.

DeeDee shook her head. "No. Sorry, Liz."

"Wait," Bill broke in. "I think I saw her going into the library a few minutes ago. Why?"

"Oh, it's nothing important. 'Bye." Without a backward glance, Elizabeth strode down the hallway toward the library. She pushed open the heavy glass doors and stepped into an oasis of peaceful silence.

Across the room, Susan sat staring out the wide picture window, looking anything but peaceful. Elizabeth crossed over to her. "Susan? Hi."

The girl looked up slowly, and Elizabeth felt a jolt in her stomach as she took in the expression of utter despair in Susan's eyes.

"What are you doing buried in here?" Elizabeth said in a light tone as she took a seat. She nodded at Susan's book. "Catching up on some homework?"

Susan looked down at the book as though she didn't know what it was or how it had gotten there. She closed her eyes briefly and tried to smile. "Oh, hi, Liz. I'm just . . ." Her words trailed off into melancholy silence.

Elizabeth regarded her for a moment, wishing there was some way she could reach out to help Susan. She drew a deep breath. "You know, I couldn't help wondering if you were feeling upset about this story that's going around," she began gently, hoping fervently that she was taking the right approach. She looked into Susan's face and saw the girl's chin tremble slightly.

"Hey, Susan, please don't be too worried," she went on, filled with pity. "There are always rumors going around, and people believe them for a while. But then they realize how wrong they are and forget all about them."

Susan looked up without speaking and shook her head dejectedly.

"Really! Remember when everyone thought I was hanging out with that horrible dropout, Rick Andover? Well, that hurt, too, but I knew that my real friends would stick by me. And they did. Just like your friends believe in *you*."

A hollow, dry laugh, almost a sob, sounded in Susan's throat. "But they don't," she moaned. "Everyone's treating me like I've got the plague."

"I'm not!"

Susan managed a faint smile. "I know. It's just that Gordon broke up with me, and I just don't understand it—I thought he really liked me!"

"I know, Susan. I'm really sorry. I guess some people aren't what you think they are."

"I just—"

"Just hang in there, Susan. This will all blow over in a couple of days, believe me. Don't worry about it."

"Sure, Liz," Susan whispered, staring out the window again.

Elizabeth looked down at her hands, feeling utterly helpless. It didn't seem as if she had done any good at all. Poor Susan was completely depressed, and it was going to take more than a cheerful "Don't worry about it" to change that.

"Listen," she said softly. "I want you to know that if you need someone to talk to, you can come to me. Really." Instinctively she reached for Susan's hand and squeezed it. A faint glimmer of a smile reached the girl's eyes and then disappeared.

"Thanks, Liz," she whispered.

There wasn't much more she could do now, Elizabeth knew. Holding back a sigh, she got to her feet. " 'Bye."

Susan nodded.

With a heavy heart, Elizabeth walked back to the library entrance. She glanced back as she opened the doors and shook her head sadly.

When she stepped out into the hall, she found herself face to face with Allen Walters. "Oh, Allen!" she exclaimed, flooded with relief. "Am I glad to see you!"

He grinned shyly. "That's nice to hear."

"Listen." She took his arm and led him a few steps away, glancing back over her shoulder. "Susan is in there, and she really needs a friend right now. She's incredibly depressed."

A strange look crossed Allen's face as she spoke. It was a combination of anger, concern, and hope all rolled into one, and Elizabeth felt her spirits lift slightly. Something told her that if anyone could help Susan, it was Allen Walters. "Will you go talk to her?"

He frowned. "You'd better believe it," he answered, his voice strong with conviction. He had never looked less shy and hesitant. "Thanks for letting me know."

With a satisfied nod, Elizabeth watched the tall boy push open the library doors. She knew Susan was in good hands now.

Allen paused inside the door when he caught sight of Susan. He suddenly felt less confident that he could really do anything to help. After all, he didn't have all that much experience with girls. He had gone with Robin Wilson, but since she broke up with him, he hadn't done much socializing. It was just too painful. For a while he had thought he'd be better off not dating at all. But then there was Susan.

He gazed at her adoringly. She was so beautiful. But there was more than that. She was friendly, down to earth, and honest—qualities he greatly admired. In his eyes she was the most wonderful girl in the world.

But he was convinced that she could never feel the same way about him. It was hopeless to dream that way, he thought. But he could still be her friend. Squaring his shoulders resolutely, he crossed the hushed library and sat down by her without speaking.

Finally she became aware of his presence, and she turned slowly to meet his gaze. "Allen," she said with a heart-melting smile. She looked surprised to see him. But glad, too.

"Hi, Susan. How's it going?"

She shook her head ruefully. "Not so great, I guess. I'm a social outcast."

"Well, that has its advantages, you know."

"It does?" She looked at him curiously.

He nodded. "Sure. Take me, for example. I don't have a whole lot of social commitments, so I have a lot more time than most people to do the things I really want to do."

He hardly dared to look at her, but he thought maybe his plan was working. She was thinking

112

about something besides the ugly rumors now, and everything depended on his ability to take her mind off those.

She appeared to be considering what he had said, as though it made some sense to her. "You've got a point there."

"See? I told you." He smiled, masking the turmoil he felt inside as he tried to think of his next words. He knew he had to step carefully to avoid turning her off again. "Tell me. What would you do if you could do anything at all?"

A look of concentration passed over her face, and then she smiled bashfully. Looking up, she said shyly, "No—I can't tell you. It's too dumb."

"Come on, sure you can. Tell me."

"Well, Aunt Helen, my guardian, is a waitress, you know. And, well, I always thought it would be kind of fun. Lots of kids do that as a summer job at the resorts—like at Palm Springs. And, well . . ."

He grinned. "Well, what do you know? You're a real person, Susan!"

At that she laughed outright. "OK, I know it's dumb. But I get tired of being the one who gets waited on at fancy restaurants all the time. Just once I'd like to be on the other side and not have to be constantly—oh, you know."

Their eyes met for a long, meaningful moment. Then Susan went on, with only a hint of wistfulness, "I guess I don't have to worry about that anymore."

"Hey, I have a great idea," Allen said hastily, pulling her away from the danger zone. "How about going with me to this coffeehouse I know near the college? It's always really dark and crowded, and you can never get a table, and the waiters are really rude to you. But there's always good music, and nobody cares who you are. How about it?" He swallowed hard. He couldn't believe he had just asked the girl of his dreams out on a date.

And he couldn't believe she was smiling at him. "That sounds like fun, Allen. I'd love to."

"Great! How about next Saturday night? A week from tomorrow?"

Her face fell, and he knew he had blundered. "That's the night of the Bridgewater Ball," she said quietly. Then she drew a deep breath and lifted her chin defiantly. "But since I'm not going to it, sure! I think that's exactly the right night to go to a coffeehouse. It'll be a lot better than making polite conversation with a bunch of old bores and smiling until my face feels like it'll fall off!"

"That's the spirit," Allen cried, lighting up with enthusiasm. "Just you wait, Susan. You'll love it. And we could eat dinner first at this diner I know—"

"OK! OK!" Susan said with a delighted laugh. "It sounds perfect!"

Allen paused and wondered briefly if he were imagining all this. But no. It was real. He simply couldn't believe Susan had said yes. His mind raced as he began to make plans for the next weekend. Polish the car, that was the first thing to do. And get a haircut? Probably. And—

Susan interrupted his thoughts. "It's time for class," she said with another one of her heart-stopping smiles. "See you later?"

"Sure. Sure, Susan. 'Bye. And, thanks!"

He sat in a happy daze as she collected her books and walked out of the library. He had done a lot more than cheer Susan up, he realized jubilantly. Asking her out was a move of sheer desperation, anything to change the subject. If he'd had time to think about it, he wouldn't have dared. But somewhere along the way he had made himself the happiest guy in Sweet Valley!

Ten

Helen Reister brushed vigorously at her thick, auburn hair, her eyes distant. The vision she saw was so far away it was impossible to reach, and she knew it. Slowly she focused on her reflection in the dresser mirror and saw the look of sadness in her eyes. Her hand dropped to her side, and her shoulders sagged.

"What should I do?" she said with a sigh, pleading forlornly for an answer. "What should I *do*?"

Her heart heavy, she sat down on her bed. When Susan had asked her the previous day for the truth, it was obvious that she desperately *needed* to know. A teenage girl had enough trouble finding out *what* she was without the extra burden of not knowing *who* she was. Was it really fair of her to hold back something that important, that critical?

But even though she realized what pain Susan was in, she couldn't bring herself to tell the truth. Although it was all she could do to resist Susan's entreaty, she *had* to refuse. She couldn't bear the thought of Susan's reaction to the truth.

She looked down at her work-worn hands. Years and years of waiting tables and stitching hems had taken their toll on the once delicate, graceful hands. It had been a long, hard road, but she *had* done the right thing. Hadn't she?

Suddenly her shoulders began to shake, and a sob escaped her lips. "Oh, Susan! Susan, my baby!" She covered her face with her hands, trying to shut out a cruel, unforgiving world. "Susan, will you ever understand?"

With a new sense of determination, Helen Reister rose to her feet and crossed the small, immaculate bedroom to her writing desk. She hesitated only for a second, then sat down, and took out a sheet of stationery and a pen. She began to write.

My darling Susan,

You'll never know how hard this is for me, but it's time you knew the truth. *I am your mother*, even though I've led you to believe otherwise for so many, many years. And you have to know why I did it.

I was never married to your father. We were both young and very much in love.

But he was very truthful with me and said he could not offer me marriage. He was at the start of a career that he knew would consume every ounce of his strength and commitment. I accepted it, but I still loved him and wanted his child.

I came to Sweet Valley after you were born and let it be known that I was merely your guardian. I didn't do it to deceive or hurt anyone, though! Please believe me. And least of all, you. But back then, how could an unmarried woman raise her child without being shunned or scorned? I couldn't let you grow up with that kind of stigma. I didn't want you to have to go through life ashamed of yourself or of me.

I thought I would tell you before now, but somehow I couldn't. And then you became so popular with the people who could help you get ahead, give you all the wonderful things I wanted for you but couldn't provide. How could I tell you then that your mother was only a waitress? I knew your best hope was for you not to know, to keep believing that you were really a princess in disguise, or something just as good.

She stopped suddenly. As her eyes traveled back up the page, reliving the long, harsh years in the words she had written, she became afraid.

Afraid of what her beautiful, laughing, graceful daughter would say when she read the letter.

With a burst of violent energy, Mrs. Reister crumpled the letter into a tight ball, and the tears streamed unchecked down her careworn face. "I can't do it!" she sobbed, clutching the balled-up paper to her heart. "I can't!"

For several minutes she sat there, pouring out the years of loneliness, hard work, and self-denial. Then, with a tremendous effort, she pulled herself together and forced herself to stop crying.

Her hands shaking, she brushed away the last stray tears and pushed herself up from the desk. Then she walked stiffly to the bathroom and smoothed the paper flat. In stony silence she ripped the letter again and again until it was just a handful of tiny shreds. She dropped them into the wastebasket and turned away.

When Susan was eighteen—that would be soon enough to tell her the truth. She would be leaving home, going off to college. It would be better then, when she was starting off on a new life, Helen Reister told herself firmly. Better for both of them.

Better—or easier? a nagging voice inside her whispered.

Defiantly she lifted her chin. "Maybe it *is* the coward's way out," she said in a defensive tone. "But I can't afford to do anything else. I have to lose Susan some day. Just let me keep her a little longer."

For a few more minutes, she stood in the bathroom, trying to compose herself. It would be terrible if Susan came home and found her in this condition, her face red and blotched with tears, her hands shaking. She leaned over the sink and splashed cool water onto her face and wrists.

The doorbell rang as she dried herself off, and she walked through the small, well-kept house with a growing sense of dread. As calmly as she could, she opened the front door. A tall, sandy-haired man stood there, a nervous, hopeful expression in his gentle eyes.

"Hello, Jackson," she said quietly. "I had a feeling you would come."

Eleven

"May I come in?" Jackson Croft asked, a faint smile on his lips.

"Of course."

She stepped aside, then followed him silently into the living room. Helen Reister indicated a chair, and Jackson Croft sat down and crossed his long legs. For a moment, neither of them spoke, regarding each other solemnly after their long separation.

"You've hardly changed at all in seventeen years," he said at last.

She shook her head sadly. "I'm afraid you're just being the gallant knight, as usual, Jackson. But you look as though life has treated you pretty well."

Pressing his lips together briefly, he looked

away. When he met her eyes again, he sighed. "Well . . ."

Another silence fell between them, and Helen Reister realized with a surge of compassion that Jackson Croft was struggling hard to remain in control of his emotions. Then she remembered what she had read in the newspapers, and she knew he must be consumed with grief.

"Jackson, I'm—I'm so sorry about your boy. It must have been the most. . . ." There could be no words to describe the pain he had been through.

"Well, that's life, right?" he said with a harsh, bitter laugh.

"Jackson, don't—don't pretend with me."

He met her warm brown eyes evenly and blinked away a tear. "You're right. You always did know exactly what I was thinking. Sorry, Helen."

"Don't be." She smiled tenderly. "What was he like? Tell me."

The man exhaled slowly. "Like? He was like—like an angel, Helen. So bright, so beautiful . . ."

"Oh, Jackson!"

"No. I'm all right—I want to talk about him, Helen. It helps me to keep—" He paused, pressing his fist to his chin. "He made me so happy, you know? It was easy to forget that there was— someone else."

She looked away and then quickly stood up and crossed to the window.

"But after I lost him I thought—how stupid of me and how selfish to have missed the chance of watching Susan grow up, sharing her life! I had to come, Helen. I—can I see her?"

She said nothing, and he stood up, too. "Helen, I know what you must think of me—"

"Do you? Do you really, Jackson? I don't think so." Turning swiftly she met his eyes, and her own eyes blazed with an intense inner fire. "I wrote to you when I moved here, hoping you would come and get me. And then I saw in the papers that you'd married. So I decided to let you get on with your life, let you forget about us. That's why I never wrote again."

"Helen—"

"Wait!" Swallowing painfully, she shook her head. "And, Jackson, I've never regretted that decision! Never! It's been tough—oh, God, has it been tough!" She whirled around to face the window again, trying to gain control of her emotions. Seeing Jackson Croft again brought everything back with stunning clarity, everything she had worked so hard to put out of her mind.

Without a word, he rested his hand on her shoulder. It was the touch of an old friend, full of understanding and sympathy. They stood that way in silence for several minutes.

Finally she walked back to the sofa and sat down, looking up at him, waiting for him to go on, to put into words what they both knew he was there for.

"I'll never forgive myself for letting myself believe you could manage on your own—even though I know you have," he said. He sat next to her and took her hand. "You know I still can't offer—"

"I know," she cut in quickly. "I don't want you to feel you owe me anything."

The famous film director, used to controlling Hollywood's biggest studios, was afraid, unsure of his footing. "But—Susan?" he asked hesitantly.

Her heart began to pound, and she rose to her feet unsteadily. "How about a drink?" she asked, suddenly desperate to lead the conversation where it had to go.

He nodded heavily.

"Is wine all right?" She hurried to the tiny kitchen with relief when he gave another weary nod. She was grateful for something to do with her hands, but the wineglasses rattled together, and she put them down hastily on the counter, afraid of breaking them. Breathing shakily, she pressed her hands together to steady them.

"Red or white?" she called out.

"White is fine."

She drew a deep breath. *Just pretend this is a normal conversation*, she told herself. *Relax. Pretend we're just talking about the weather.* With a calm that surprised her, she poured two glasses of white wine and carried them back to the living room.

When she walked into the room, Jackson Croft was holding a framed photograph of Susan. Helen Reister set the drinks down carefully on the coffee table.

"She's—she's very beautiful," he said quietly.

She nodded.

"She takes after you."

There was a tense silence, and Helen Reister felt her throat tightening as tears threatened to come. "Please don't, Jackson."

"I'm sorry." He drew a deep breath. "Another woman might have come to me by now for help. I—I have a lot of money, you know." He looked sheepish, as though he were embarrassed to have been so successful at his work.

But all she could do was shake her head mutely. Finally she forced herself to speak. "Why have you come, Jackson? Really?"

He rubbed his forehead, an old gesture she remembered well. "I thought I could—she could—I thought maybe . . ." He stopped, unable to find the right words. "If I could see her, talk to her, tell her why I—"

"Wait!" Reaching unsteadily for her glass,

Helen Reister tried to calm herself again. She felt she was swimming underwater and running out of air. "She doesn't know anything about you," she said carefully. "I'd rather tell her myself, and then you could see her. Please? Let me explain first. Then you can come back."

She must have sounded nearly desperate, because a look of pain and pity came into the man's eyes as she spoke. He nodded slowly. "I understand, Helen."

A tiny sigh of relief escaped her, and she sipped tiredly at her wine. She had never felt so exhausted in all her life. They sat quietly for a moment, falling into an old familiar pattern of silent communication.

Suddenly they heard footsteps on the front porch, and before either of them could move, the door swung open and Susan walked in with a cheerful smile. She stopped when she saw them, an inquiring look on her face. Then she took in the wineglasses, and her eyebrows drew together. She frowned, puzzled.

"Susan," Jackson Croft said huskily, his face flushed. He rose to his feet and took a step toward her.

Her eyes widened with recognition. "You're— Jackson Croft, aren't you?"

He nodded mutely.

A look of surprise and then alarm crossed her

128

face, and she turned to the woman she had thought of as her guardian all her life. "What's going on here?" she said, her voice rising in a frightened pitch. "What is he doing here?"

Twelve

Susan knew immediately that Mrs. Reister and Jackson Croft weren't having a casual conversation. She also knew in her heart that something momentous was about to happen to her.

A strangled, inarticulate sound came from Mrs. Reister's throat, and she suddenly fled from the room. A door slammed down the hall.

Her anxiety growing every second, Susan confronted the director. "Would you please tell me what you're doing here? What have you done to her?"

He held his wineglass in both hands and stared into its depths for a moment. Finally, he drew a deep breath and looked up, meeting her eyes steadily. "Susan, I'm your father."

"My . . . father?" she repeated. She groped blindly for a chair and lowered herself into it.

"My father?" For so long she had devoted all her hopes to finding her real mother. She had almost forgotten that somewhere she had a father, too.

"I don't understand," she whispered, staring up at him.

"Susan. I know this is kind of a shock—"

"A 'shock'?" All she could do was echo his words automatically. Her mind was numb.

He sat down across from her, leaning forward intently, his forearms on his knees. His eyes, full of hope and apprehension, scanned her face.

Father. Father. This man is my father. Susan swallowed hard and met his anxious gaze. "How—?"

"You see, I left your mother when she was pregnant," he explained in a contrite tone. "I—I didn't know she was, at the time."

He frowned, as though remembering back through the years. "I was going on an assignment to Venezuela to make a documentary about the military dictator— Oh! You don't want to hear about that!" he interrupted himself with an angry gesture.

Susan stared at him, amazed. This intense, vital man, a man respected and admired around the world for his insightful movies, was her *father.* He was clearly a man of strong passions—dedicated, committed to his work. Her mind was reeling.

"Well," he continued with a regretful smile, "when I got back you had been born, and your mother had gone away. I knew you were in Sweet Valley. I kept telling myself I'd come and get you, but I kept putting it off, and then I married Veronica—" He stopped talking for a moment, then said, "There's no excuse for what I did, Susan. I can't ask you to forgive me."

She nodded slowly. "Your son died."

He gave her a piercing look. "You know that's why I came." It was a statement of fact rather than a question. Already there was a bond of understanding between them.

"Anyway, I hope maybe we can see something of each other," he continued. "I've neglected you for too long."

As she looked at him, she began to see something of herself in his face, and her heart swelled with emotion. "I'd like that," she whispered, unsure of her exact feelings. But she knew she meant it.

Relief washed over his face. "That's great, Susan. Maybe you could even come to L.A. and stay with us. Veronica knows all about you, and she'd love to meet you. And I'm sure your mother wouldn't mind."

Susan gasped; she felt almost dizzy. "My mother? But, I mean—who?"

Jackson Croft's forehead creased in a puzzled frown. "What do you mean? What about her?"

"Who—is—she?" The words dropped out like tiny stones. She stared at him, imploring him for the answer she was afraid to hear.

"I don't understand, Susan." He looked at her in obvious confusion, and she saw his eyes move to stare at the doorway behind her.

She turned slowly in her seat. Mrs. Reister stood framed in the door of the hallway, shaking her head. An expression of sheer anguish was etched on the woman's face.

Jackson Croft cleared his throat. "Helen, doesn't she know?" he whispered, his voice filled with incredulity.

The woman still shook her head, staring wordlessly into Susan's eyes.

As Susan met her guardian's steady gaze, the haze of misunderstanding cleared, as if blown away by a cold, sharp wind. She felt she couldn't catch her breath. She stumbled to her feet. "You're my mother!" she choked out, her hand rising to her throat.

The auburn hair. The large brown eyes. The finely molded cheekbones. How could she have been so blind? All the years of waiting and hoping and wondering, and her mother had been there all the time!

A hot flush flooded Susan's face, and then the blood drained away, leaving her faint and dizzy again. "Why?" she whispered, tears spilling from her eyes. "Why have you lied to me all this time? I wanted a mother for so long!"

Her knees gave way and buckled underneath her. She felt herself caught in a pair of strong arms, and her father lifted her tenderly onto the couch and put his arms around her. She rested her head against his shoulder and sobbed. In a few short minutes her life had been turned completely inside out, and she didn't think she could cope with all the changes.

"Susan, shhh. It's OK," Jackson Croft whispered, rocking her gently in his arms. "It's OK. Just let it all out."

After what seemed like an eternity, Susan raised her head and looked around in a daze. She and Jackson Croft were alone in the living room.

"Where—?"

"I think she's in her room," he said softly, looking into her eyes with grave concern.

Susan shook her head. It felt two sizes too large, and her ears were ringing from her crying. "How could she do that to me?" she demanded, her indignant anger beginning to mount. "Why would she pretend all this time that she was just my guardian when she *knew* how much I wanted to have a mother? I don't understand!"

Her father took her hand and prevented her from jumping up off the couch. "Wait a minute, Susan. I think I know why. It was a brave thing to do."

"Brave? Brave to lie to me and break my heart? Come on!"

"Susan, listen to me!" His voice was stern, commanding. "Put yourself in her position. She was a young woman with no husband. She had you. Maybe she had seen the way kids with no fathers were treated. Maybe she didn't want you to go through life feeling like a—"

She shook her head, trying to make sense of it all. It was too much! She couldn't take it all in.

"And I think it goes to show just how much she loves you, too," he went on, his voice low and intense. "She had to give up your love in order to give you what she could. That must have been a terrible sacrifice. Think about it, Susan. Think what she gave up for you."

Her chin trembling, she met his eyes. "You know, when I was little, I used to wish she were my mother. She was so kind and gentle, and she loved me so much. I never let myself love her as much as I wanted to because I thought I had to save it for my real mother. But I wanted her to be my mother so I could love her."

With a tender smile, he touched her cheek. "I think she'd probably like to hear that," he said softly.

All the pieces came tumbling into place as Susan sat there. There was no mysterious person sending them money. Her mother did provide the money, but by waitressing. Sewing.

Working for *her*. And all the time, she had taken her "Aunt Helen" for granted, thought she was working because she wanted something extra. But everything came from her hard work. Every last cent that Susan had spent so *carelessly* on new clothes and tennis lessons.

"Oh, God." She sighed. "I'm so—so—"

Jackson Croft stood up. "Susan, I came here because I want you to come and live with me if you want to. I need you to be part of my life. You know I'd do anything for you. But right now, I think there's somebody who needs you even more than I do."

She looked up blankly. He raised his eyebrows and pulled her to her feet. "Go on. Go to your mother."

"I can't," she whispered. "I'm so ashamed."

With his hands on her shoulders, he turned around and pointed her down the hallway. "Yes, you can," he said with a gentle push.

She stood there as if paralyzed for another few moments. The front door clicked shut behind her, and she knew she was alone. But down the hall was a brave, good woman who had given everything she had to Susan. And that woman was her mother.

"Can you ever forgive me?"

Susan looked into Mrs. Reister's eyes. "Oh,

Aunt Helen—Mother," she corrected herself with a shy smile.

Tears sprang to Mrs. Reister's eyes again, and she brushed them away. "Gee, you would have thought I couldn't cry anymore," she said in an attempt at lightness.

After Susan had steeled herself to face her real mother, she had walked into Mrs. Reister's bedroom. One look, and the two were in each other's arms crying and laughing and hugging to make up for lost time.

"It's like a dream come true," Susan said, taking her mother's hand and looking into her eyes. "I found my real mother at last, and she turned out to be the most wonderful person in the whole world."

"No, don't say that, darling. I've made so many mistakes in my life."

They stared at each other for another long moment. Susan felt as though her heart would explode with happiness. "I even got a father at the same time," she said, still marvelling at the incredible chain of events that had changed her life.

Mrs. Reister looked gravely at her daughter. "He's a good man, Susan. Don't think badly of him."

"I—I guess I don't. He—" She broke off, unsure if she should tell her mother about Jackson Croft's invitation to move to L.A. and live with him.

"He asked you to go with him, didn't he?"

Susan nodded mutely, searching her mother's face. "But I can't go," she admitted. "Not now. Now when I've finally found you. I can't leave you now."

"Oh, Susan."

The girl brushed away another happy tear. "I've got to start paying you back for all the good things you've done for me all my life," she said, smiling through her tears. "And it's going to take a long time, so I'd better get started—Mother."

"You don't need to repay me for anything, darling," her mother whispered. "All I ever want from you is for you to be happy, you know that."

"I am happy now. I don't think I've ever been happier in my whole life."

Silently, mother and daughter embraced, communicating their love to each other without words. Then Susan raised her head and looked into the gentle brown eyes that were so like her own. "I have to tell you something."

Mrs. Reister tenderly brushed aside a lock of Susan's hair. "What is it?"

Ducking her head with a bashful smile, Susan confessed, "When I was little I used to wish that whoever my real mother was would go away and leave me alone with you so—so you could be my mother. Maybe I knew somehow

139

that you were the one I needed, the one I loved. I wished every night that you would be my mother."

Tears sprang to Mrs. Reister's eyes again, and her lips quivered with a joyful smile. "You got your wish then, didn't you?"

Susan nodded, her heart full. "I guess dreams can come true, after all."

"Liz! Emergency!"

"What? What is it?" Elizabeth looked up from the book she was reading. Jessica's emergencies usually involved running out of Diet Coke or finding a split end.

"Tomorrow is the most important day of my life, Liz. And I don't know *what* to wear."

Elizabeth rolled her eyes. "Speaking of which, where's my dress?"

"In my room," Jessica said dismissively. "But we're talking about what I should wear to the casting call, remember?"

"In your room?" her twin persisted. "On a hanger, or under your bed?"

Jessica fixed her with a look of injured dignity. "On a *hanger*, Liz. Come on! Now I really need some advice about tomorrow. What should I wear?"

"Hmm . . ." Elizabeth dropped her eyes back to the book she had been reading. She couldn't make up her mind if she would tell her sister what she had just read. On the other hand, there was no point in getting Jessica any more worked up about their mother than she already was. But on the other hand . . .

"Just wait a second, Jess. I borrowed your book from health class. I think you should hear this." As Jessica sat down on the bed, Elizabeth read aloud. " 'Women who bear twins once are statistically more likely than other women to bear twins a second time—' "

"Are you serious?" Jessica gasped, her blue-green eyes staring wildly. "You mean Mom's going to have *twins* again?"

"Not necessarily," Elizabeth hastened to say. She pulled her knees up to her chin and shook her head thoughtfully. "But we'd better be prepared for the possibility."

"Oh, God!" groaned Jessica, flopping over onto her back. "Can you imagine? Twins? Give me strength!"

Thirteen

"Hurry up! Come on, Liz!" Jessica squealed. Traffic was backing up as they neared the Hampton Place shopping center where the auditions for *La Luna* were to take place, and Jessica was squirming in her seat with impatience.

"Just let me find somewhere to park before you go leaping out of the car, all right? I don't feel like scraping you off the road." Maneuvering the girls' red Fiat convertible through the crowded lot, Elizabeth felt her own excitement mounting. Even though she herself wasn't expecting to make a break into movie stardom, she was eagerly anticipating meeting the director.

As soon as the car stopped, Jessica vaulted out and headed for the crowd. "See you later, Liz!"

"But— Oh, never mind!" Elizabeth chuckled.

She was left to put up the top by herself, but she didn't really mind.

"Hey! Need some help?" a familiar voice called out.

Looking up, Elizabeth saw Aaron Dallas and his girlfriend, Heather Sanford, weaving their way through the parked cars toward her. Aaron was Jeffrey's best friend, and recently the four of them had been through an emotional time together. Aaron's parents were in the middle of long, messy divorce proceedings, and Aaron had had a lot of trouble coping. But thanks to the support of his friends, he was learning to control his turbulent emotions.

His dark eyes crinkled at the corners as he smiled in the bright sunlight. "So where's Jeffrey?" he teased as he helped snap the Fiat's top into place. "Isn't he here for his big break?"

"Oh, you know Jeffrey," Elizabeth bantered easily. "He's too far above such mundane things. He's leaving the groveling to us today."

Heather hugged her arms around herself and shivered with excitement. "Wouldn't it be just unbelievable if someone from our school got a part?" she said breathlessly.

"My dear sister thinks she's going to be the one," Elizabeth told them wryly as she swung her bag over her shoulder. "Let's go."

The three headed across the parking lot toward a crowd of eager, would-be movie stars. It was a typical Saturday morning in Sweet Valley: absolutely gorgeous, with blazing sunshine and a gentle ocean breeze. Elizabeth couldn't repress a smile of anticipation as they drew closer. If she could get to Jackson Croft, it would be *her* lucky day, after all.

Many of her fellow classmates were milling around, chattering excitedly. Sandra Bacon and Jean West were there, talking with animated gestures to some of the other cheerleaders. And Elizabeth caught sight of Sally Larson, Dana's cousin, with her boyfriend, Mark Riley. Dana was there, too, along with the other members of The Droids.

"Hey, you guys!" Dana called, waving madly at them.

Aaron raised one eyebrow. "I think we're being summoned."

"Let's go hang out with them," Heather suggested, tugging his arm. She turned to Elizabeth. "Are you going to come with us?"

Elizabeth shook her head. "I promised to meet Enid here, and I have a feeling it's not going to be easy! Why don't you two go ahead, and we'll try to catch up with you later."

"OK. 'Bye. Oh, hey—wait a minute," Aaron said suddenly. "Regina Morrow is looking for you. She said she's got something she wants to show you."

"Do you know what?" Elizabeth asked.

But he shook his head. "No, sorry. I didn't have a chance to ask. Anyway, see you later."

Elizabeth watched as Aaron and Heather made their way through the crowd to the main Sweet Valley High contingent. Then she turned to start searching for her friend. None of the official movie people seemed to be there yet, and everyone was just milling around. She didn't know whether she should find Enid first or try to find Regina.

"Liz! Over here!" Enid called from the crowd.

"Oh, Enid!" Elizabeth gasped with relief. "It's a miracle! I'm so glad I found you!"

Enid's green eyes twinkled with amusement. "I had no idea you felt that way about me, Liz!"

"Well, don't get carried away. It's not because I like you, it's because I want to stand on your shoulders," Elizabeth said.

"Oh, I'm crushed!"

The girls laughed as they moved slowly through the outskirts of the crowd, looking for a good vantage point. "Look, there's Jessica," Enid said, pointing ahead. "And she looks furious about something!"

"Oh, great! Well, I guess we'd better go see what the problem is. No point in putting it off." As they neared her, Jessica turned and saw them. Her face immediately took on its most wrathful expression.

"You will not believe what that sneak, Lila Fowler, has done," she stormed.

Patient as usual, Elizabeth asked, "Now what?"

"She went and got that slime, Gordon Stoddard, to ask her to the Bridgewater Ball, that's what! They're together over there. Look at the way they're staring at each other. It's just revolting!"

Elizabeth and Enid exchanged expressive glances. "Hmm. Too bad, Jess. I guess you borrowed my dress for nothing, then."

Narrowing her eyes, Jessica snapped, "Well, I didn't want to go to that stupid ball anyway. And honestly! The way Lila *threw* herself at him. I can't get over— What is it? What's going on?" she interrupted herself. Half the crowd was staring in the same direction. People were pointing and talking excitedly. "Is Jackson Croft here?"

Elizabeth craned her neck and caught a glimpse of someone setting up a microphone on a makeshift platform. Two vans and a station wagon were parked behind the cleared area, and several official-looking men and women were bustling around. "I think it's them," she said breathlessly. "Let's get closer!"

But everyone else had the same idea, and the twins and Enid were stuck where they were. There was an expectant hush, and a tall, sandy-haired man stepped up onto the platform. "That must be him," Enid whispered. "He looks familiar, doesn't he?"

Elizabeth tipped her head to one side, studying his face. He did look familiar. "We must have seen pictures of him," she suggested.

"Hmm. I guess so."

Jackson Croft took the microphone from an assistant and blew into it experimentally. "Can you all hear me?" he asked with a disarming smile.

"Yes!" the crowd roared back at him.

"Great! This is probably a new experience for most of you," the director began casually. "So let me fill you in on how we'll be operating this morning. But first of all, let me tell you that no one will be cast today. If we want you to come back, we'll ask for your name, and we'll contact you later."

As the man spoke, Elizabeth listened with growing admiration. He seemed perfectly at ease addressing such a large crowd, and he managed to convey the feeling that he was talking directly to each individual. He outlined the types of people they were looking for, then handed the microphone back to the assistant.

"First off, we'd like to see some guys for the high school football team. High school boys, please," the younger man said, consulting a clipboard. "If you'll please come up to the front here."

148

An eager ripple ran through the crowd, and boys from Sweet Valley High and other nearby schools began surging forward to the audition area. Elizabeth was keeping an eye on Croft, however, and when she saw him duck behind the vans, she grabbed Enid's arm.

"Come on," she said quietly. "Let's talk to him while everyone's watching the boys."

"I'm coming, too," Jessica announced. "Let's hurry, though."

The three girls dodged around the edge of the group, and as the assistant began to explain what the boys would be doing, they squeezed between the two vans and found themselves standing in front of Jackson Croft. He was sitting in a lawn chair, staring intently at a sheaf of papers.

"Excuse me," Elizabeth began, twisting her hands together nervously.

Jackson Croft looked up with a start and raised his eyebrows inquisitively. "We'll be seeing girls in a few minutes," he said with an apologetic smile.

"Oh, I know, but that's not why I came," she continued. "I write for our school newspaper, and I was wondering if I could interview you about—" Elizabeth broke off, her face burning.

"About my movies?"

"No, not exactly." Elizabeth looked frantically at Enid for support. She knew that part of being a good journalist meant asking tough questions, but she didn't want to say the wrong thing and make the director angry.

"I—I read that you're donating your profits—to Students Against Drunk Driving," she said hesitantly, hardly daring to meet his eyes.

"I see."

She gulped. *You blew it!* she raged silently.

"I'd be glad to talk to you," Jackson Croft said quietly. "What school do you go to?"

"Sweet Valley High." She gasped. Suddenly she became aware of Jessica and Enid fidgeting behind her. "I'm Elizabeth Wakefield, and this is my sister, Jessica, and my friend Enid Rollins. We're all big fans of yours."

"That's right," Jessica put in, stepping forward to shake the director's hand. "And I think I'd be terrific in your movie," she said with a bold smile."

"Jessica!"

Jackson Croft held up his hand. "That's all right, Elizabeth. I can see your sister has the makings of a real celebrity."

For once in her life, Jessica Wakefield was stunned completely speechless. She blushed to the roots of her hair, opened her mouth, but nothing came out.

"So, you go to Sweet Valley High," he went on, hiding a smile at Jessica's discomfiture. "Is that a good school?"

150

Elizabeth and Enid looked at each other. "Sure. It's a very good school," Enid said in a surprised voice.

He nodded slowly and seemed to forget about them for a moment. Staring into space, he rubbed his forehead and frowned. The three girls looked at one another uneasily.

"Mr. Croft?" Elizabeth whispered.

"Hmm? Oh, sorry, girls." He gave them a friendly smile and stood up. "Let me get you something to sit on."

Before they knew what was happening, he had reached into the van and pulled out some more folding chairs. "Here you go," he said, opening the chairs and setting them down. "Now, Elizabeth, fire away."

Elizabeth opened her mouth. "Right now? I mean, you want to do the interview right now?"

He threw his head back and laughed. "Yes, by all means." His eyes twinkled as he looked at her surprised face.

"Wow!" She dug into her purse for the pen and notebook she always carried with her and assumed her most professional journalistic manner. "Now—" she began, and then stopped. She couldn't think of a single question.

Jackson Croft smiled politely, but then his eyes widened, as he stared at something behind her. He sprang to his feet, knocking his chair over backward. "Susan!"

All three girls spun around in their chairs to see Susan Stewart looking nervously at the director. Elizabeth knew she was staring—so were Jessica and Enid—in total surprise. Not only did Jackson Croft seem to know Susan, but he was obviously very excited to see her.

"I had to talk to you," Susan began, oblivious of the other three girls. "I had to tell you that I can't—I can't—"

Elizabeth watched, wide-eyed. It didn't take a reporter's instinct to know that something big was going on. She could scarcely comprehend the scene unfolding in front of her.

"You talked to your mother."

Susan nodded, looking at him with wide, apologetic eyes. "I'd love to come to stay with you, visit you in L.A. for a while, but I can't leave her now. Maybe I'll come soon, but right now, I've got to stay with her. So much has happened."

Jackson Croft gave her a sad, regretful smile. "I guess I knew you would say that. But you will come—soon? Now that I've found you—"

"*Mr. Croft!*" a voice boomed over the loud-speaker. "*Please see Diane Baxter immediately!*"

He stared at Susan for another moment. "I'll be right back," he said brusquely, clearly annoyed by the interruption. "Stay here, though, OK?" Then he slipped between the vans and disappeared.

Susan Stewart exhaled slowly and suddenly became aware of her audience. "I guess you're kind of wondering . . ."

"Susan!" Jessica gasped. "You never told anyone you knew him! And just what did he mean about you coming to visit him in L.A.?" she asked suspiciously.

Elizabeth glared at her twin and stood up, pushing Susan into her chair. It was obvious to her that the girl was under an enormous emotional strain. "Just ignore her, Susan."

"It's like a dream," the girl said quietly. "He's my father, you know."

A stunned silence greeted this announcement. "Your *father*?" Enid repeated incredulously.

"Yes. I just found out yesterday." Susan looked up and met Elizabeth's eyes, and in a low, dazed voice, she related everything that had happened the day before.

"Pretty amazing, huh?" she finished, giving them a smile.

Elizabeth reached out impulsively and hugged the redhead. "I'm so happy for you, Susan. I know how much this must mean to you."

"Yes," Enid added. "You deserve it, Susan."

She smiled at them both. "It's going to take some getting used to," she admitted. "But it's an adjustment I'm glad to make."

Elizabeth drew a deep breath. Who would

153

ever have dreamed . . . ? Suddenly she noticed that her sister had disappeared.

"Where's Jess?"

Enid and Susan looked surprised. "I guess she left," Enid said.

The three girls exchanged a meaningful glance. "Well," Elizabeth concluded, "I guess by now everyone in Sweet Valley knows your story, Susan. Sorry."

"That's OK," Susan answered with a happy smile. "I want the whole world to know how lucky I am!"

Later that afternoon, Elizabeth and Jessica met their brother at the beach for an emergency strategy meeting. Jessica carefully massaged cocoa butter onto her long bronzed legs and listened while Steven and Elizabeth discussed "the situation." The movie people hadn't asked them for her name, so she knew she wasn't going to get a call-back for *La Luna*. Even though she was disappointed, she was going to put the whole thing out of her mind and refocus her attention on her mother.

"The way I see it," Steven was saying, "they're just trying to stall as long as possible. They don't know how to break it to us, so they keep putting it off."

Elizabeth agreed. "Maybe they're waiting for the right moment."

"That's my whole point! They keep waiting, and the right moment doesn't come! I say we *make* it be the right moment!"

Jessica scooped up a handful of sand and poured it out in a thin stream. "So what are you saying, Steve? How do we make it the right moment?"

"I say we go home and tell them that we know all about it. Just tell them."

"Are you sure?" Elizabeth asked, the note of doubt in her voice obvious.

Jessica looked out at the sparkling Pacific Ocean. "Steve's right," she said thoughtfully. She nodded firmly. "It's up to us."

"Well, if you both think it's the right thing to do . . ."

Jumping to his feet, Steven gave them both a big smile. "Definitely. Let's go home and do it right now!"

The three of them raced across the sand and climbed into Steven's yellow Volkswagen. Within minutes they were pulling up in front of their house. Both their parents' cars were there.

"It's now or never," Steven said grimly. "Let's go for it!"

They found their parents out by the pool. Mr. Wakefield looked up from his newspaper. "What's

155

this?" he asked with a grin as his son and daughters lined up in front of them.

"Mom, Dad, we've got to talk."

Jessica looked at Steven, grateful that he was taking control of the situation.

"Mmm. Sounds serious," Mrs. Wakefield said lightly. "What is it?"

"We know everything."

The look of surprise their parents exchanged seemed to confirm their speculations. Obviously they were taken off guard.

Nodding slowly, Mrs. Wakefield said, "You do, huh?"

Elizabeth held out her hands. "We want you to know that we're really happy about it. So you don't have to hide it anymore."

Mr. and Mrs. Wakefield looked at each other again. Finally Mrs. Wakefield looked back at her children. "Something tells me I'm going to regret this, but just what are we hiding that you're so happy about?"

Steven let out an exasperated sigh. "The *baby*, Mom. We know."

Her mouth dropped open. "The—what?"

"I'm sure he said *baby*," Mr. Wakefield said. "But just why he said it, I haven't the vaguest idea."

Jessica began to feel a peculiar sensation in her stomach, and she caught a quick look of alarm from her twin. "Mom, we *know* you're pregnant," she said.

Mrs. Wakefield gasped. "What on earth ever gave you that idea?"

The sensation in Jessica's stomach became even more peculiar. "Mom—"

"Are you saying you're not?" Steven demanded, his face flaming red.

Mrs. Wakefield shook her head, a perplexed smile on her face. "No, I'm not!"

"But, Mom," Elizabeth said nervously, "you've been talking about—about names, and getting cravings for pistachio ice cream—"

Her father's hoot of laughter stopped her in midsentence. "And that made you think your mother was pregnant?"

Elizabeth blushed fiercely. "Yes." She darted another look at Jessica. "But it wasn't my idea to begin with," she said menacingly.

A jolt of panic rippled through Jessica. Something told her she was about to be pounced on. "Wait a minute!" she protested, turning frantically to her mother again. "I found baby clothes in your closet! How do you explain that?"

"I'm going to a baby shower next week. And how do you explain digging around in my closet, young lady?"

Jessica didn't answer; she was still trying to figure out what was going on. "And we heard you and Daddy talking about not telling us

157

something until it was definite," she went on wildly. "What was that all about?"

Her parents exchanged another surprised look. "Something tells me we've been under surveillance," Mr. Wakefield said dryly. He looked at Jessica again. "We were discussing the possibility of taking a month-long vacation and leaving you girls here by yourselves. That's all."

Suddenly Mrs. Wakefield began to laugh. "Now it all makes sense. All this bizarre talk about babies—I thought all three of you were going insane!"

Jessica stood by helplessly as Elizabeth and Steven glared at her. Then they both turned around and stalked back into the house.

She turned to her parents with a sheepish grin. "Oops."

They burst out laughing. "Oh, Jessica!" Her father chuckled. "You've really done it this time!"

Fourteen

The Beach Disco reverberated with the beat of a driving dance tune, but out on the deck a group of people were sitting at a large table, and laughter filled the surf-scented night air. "And that is the story of how our mother is *not* pregnant," Elizabeth concluded with a flourish. She grinned at her brother as she added, "Yet another one of Jessica's famous fiascos, which we are all familiar with."

"That's really not fair," Jessica objected. "It was really all Lila's fault."

"What?" Lila popped her soda straw out of her mouth. "How did I end up being the one to blame?"

Jessica pointed an accusing finger at her friend. "You were the one who kept blabbing on and on about how young my mother is and how perfectly normal it would be!"

"Oh, give me a break, Jessica!"

"Yeah," Cara cut in. She smiled up at Steven, who had his arm around her shoulders. "It looks like you're the jumper-to-conclusions here, Jess."

"Whose side are you on, anyway?" Jessica looked glumly at Cara. "Traitor."

Jeffrey ran his index finger up Elizabeth's arm in a way that made her shiver with delight. "What I can't figure out is how this one fell for it."

"Hook, line, and sinker!" Winston laughed and gave them all a broad wink.

With a playful punch on his shoulder, Maria teased, "You would have, too. You're really a sentimental slob."

Elizabeth shrugged and sent her boyfriend a rueful smile. "Oh, well. What can I say? But you have to admit, my sister can be pretty convincing!"

"Hear, hear!" shouted Winston, pounding the table with his fist amid the general laughter of assent.

"OK, OK, I admit it," Jessica said with a modest smile. "But life around here would be pretty dull without me, wouldn't it?"

"I refuse to answer on the grounds that it

might incriminate me," Steven announced severely. "Don't push your luck, Sis."

"I'm surprised you can laugh about it so soon," Enid murmured in Elizabeth's ear. "I'd still be planning her murder if I were you."

Elizabeth smiled. "Oh, well. I figure it'll make a good idea for a book someday. All in the name of literature, I guess!" She sighed contentedly and looked out over the railing. It was a perfect night, clear and balmy, and she was really enjoying spending it at the disco with all her friends.

"Say, Jess," Winston teased. "I simply cannot believe you didn't get a part in the movie. Personally, I'm ready to cut my throat, I'm so disappointed."

"That would be doing us all a favor," Lila drawled with a sly smile.

Jessica shrugged airily. "Oh, well, that's show business. It's not my fault if they can't spot talent when it comes up and stares them in the face."

Now that the connection between Jackson Croft and Susan Stewart had been discovered, Elizabeth suspected that the movie had been just an excuse for the director to come to Sweet Valley. She didn't really blame him, though. It must have been a pretty difficult thing to do.

Even as her thoughts returned to the incredible scene at the morning's auditions, she saw

Susan step outside onto the deck. "Susan!" she called, waving at the girl. "Over here!"

Susan came over, and as people made room for her, she took a seat. "Whew! I haven't danced so much in ages," she said breathlessly. "It's incredible how nice everyone's being to me tonight."

Now that you're famous again, Elizabeth added in silent sympathy. People were so calculating. They only liked Susan because of who she was and what they could get from her, not because of what kind of a person she was.

And Susan Stewart deserved to be liked for herself, if anyone did, Elizabeth thought. What a shame so many people ignored the real Susan and saw only the daughter of Jackson Croft, famous director. That was probably what had been happening all day. Elizabeth felt as sorry for the girl now as she had when everyone had turned their backs on her.

"Elizabeth, you'll never believe what happened just now," Susan told her, an excited smile lighting her face. "I was dancing with Gordon, and he said he realized what a terrible mistake he'd made, and could I still go to the Bridgewater Ball with him. Isn't that great?"

"What?" Lila choked on her soda as she overheard the announcement.

Susan turned wide eyes to Lila. "Yes! I can't believe it!"

Lila's voice was quavering with anger as she said, "Neither can I."

Shocked and disappointed, Elizabeth stared at Susan. After the way Gordon had treated her, was she still willing to go to the dance with him? And of all the despicable things—he *had* asked Lila, after all. How was he planning to get out of that?

And furthermore, Elizabeth remembered Allen Walters telling her proudly that he was taking Susan out the night of the ball. Was Susan going to stand him up after all he'd done for her?

Agitated, she pushed her straw into the crushed ice at the bottom of her root beer. "Susan," she began hesitantly, "it's none of my business, but I thought Allen . . ." She trailed off, blushing.

A cloud passed over Susan's face. "Oh"—her voice sounded small—"maybe . . . I think he just asked me out of pity, don't you? He knew I was feeling so alone. . ." She dropped her eyes from Elizabeth's questioning gaze.

She opened her mouth to speak again, but suddenly Allen was there, smiling as he looked down at her.

"Hi," he said, taking a seat next to her. "Susan, congratulations about everything."

"Allen! Thanks, I—about our date—"

"That's what I wanted to talk to you about,"

he cut in eagerly, pulling his chair closer. "I found out about this new Japanese restaurant where they cut the food up and cook it right in front of you. I know it's really corny and everything, but—"

The expression of dismay on her face pulled him up short, and he flushed painfully. "Oh, I guess you'll probably be too busy now, going to Hollywood parties and meeting interesting people," he said. He got to his feet awkwardly. "I can understand how you wouldn't want to bother with a guy like me."

"Allen! Would you shut up!" Susan laughed suddenly as she grabbed his arm to pull him back down.

He looked at her speechlessly.

"The most important and interesting thing on my schedule is to go out with you," she said, giving Elizabeth a warm smile. "I know who my real friends are now, Allen. And you're the best of them all."

His joyful expression made her laugh, and she squeezed his hand. "How about a dance?"

They stood and crossed the deck to the dance-floor door. Just then, Gordon Stoddard stepped outside and ran into them. The anxious frown on his face disappeared when he saw her.

"Susan! There you are. I was just—"

"Gordon, I completely forgot. I'm busy the night of the ball, and I'll be busy every night from now on. So you can take your snobbery and your stupid Bridgewater Ball and go jump into the ocean with it! Goodbye." Susan turned and took an awestruck Allen Walters by the arm and led him back into the disco.

Gordon opened and shut his mouth several times, a look of pure amazement on his face as he watched their retreating figures. When he turned around, he saw everyone watching him expectantly. And he saw Lila, murder in her eyes.

"Lila!" he cried with a feeble attempt at joviality. "I've been meaning to talk to you!"

"So have I, Gordon." Mustering all her dignity, Lila stood up and walked to him, a smile frozen on her face. "And this is what I wanted to say." In an instant her hand shot out, and she tipped the contents of her soda cup over his head. Then she brushed her hands off and strode inside.

Spluttering and gasping, Gordon Stoddard stood in the middle of the deck, soda and little bits of crushed ice trickling down his face and neck. His expensive cashmere sweater was sopping wet. "Lila, I can explain!" he cried.

It was too much for the group. Everyone collapsed into laughter as Gordon turned and fled.

Jessica was laughing as hard as the rest of them. "Boy, I always knew he was a total zero," she declared. "And I guess Lila knows it now, too!"

Elizabeth chuckled, then looked up quickly when she heard her name called.

"Liz! I've been tracking you like a big-game hunter for days!" Regina Morrow, dark-haired and cover-girl beautiful, threw herself into a chair beside Elizabeth and smiled in relief. "Finally!"

"Hi, Regina. I'm sorry I couldn't find you this morning. What's up?" She turned her chair so that they were sitting apart from the rest of the crowd. The others in the group resumed speaking, not paying attention to Regina and Elizabeth's conversation.

"Well," Regina began, tucking a strand of long hair behind one ear, "I know how interested you were in the schools and everything in Switzerland, and I remembered that I had a lot of brochures and things at home. There was a possibility that I'd stay for a lot longer than I did—in case I needed more treatments," she added softly.

Elizabeth gave her a warm smile. "Well, I guess you didn't need to, right? You can hear so well."

The girl laughed. "Better than I ever dreamed! But I wanted to show you this," she continued, taking a small booklet from her purse. "This is the Interlochen School. It's a very good boarding school, and they emphasize literature and creative writing. In fact, they're famous for it."

Elizabeth's eyes were riveted on the cover of the booklet. It was a photograph of a sprawling, chalet-style building built into the side of a hill; towering, snow-capped peaks rose behind it. The window shutters had heart-shaped cutouts, and trailing, red-flowered plants grew in boxes along a wide balcony. Nearby, a curly-horned sheep grazed. She could almost hear the melodic tinkling of its bell.

"Take a look," Regina prompted with an encouraging smile. "You can get a lot out of a school like this. It would be the experience of a lifetime."

Nodding slowly, Elizabeth flipped open the booklet and scanned the text. Even a quick glance was enough to tell her that going to such a school *would* be the experience of a lifetime. If only it were possible to go! But of course, boarding school in Europe was a luxury the Wakefields couldn't possibly afford.

"Thanks, Regina," she said, regretfully handing it back. "I really appreciate your showing it to me, but there's no way my parents could afford something like this."

"Wait a minute, Liz. There are all kinds of scholarships and grants you can get! Really, you should look into it! If I were in your place, I wouldn't give up until I'd looked at all the possibilities."

Regina's words filled Elizabeth's with new hope. It *was* senseless to give up so quickly. Perhaps what she should do would be to write to the headmaster and find out exactly what her options were.

Her blue-green eyes blazed with excitement. Imagine living in Switzerland: immersing herself in another culture; traveling around Europe on holidays; studying creative writing at the Interlochen School! She turned to the list of faculty members and read the headmaster's name: Alex Hummel.

Suddenly she couldn't wait to get home. It was worth a try, Elizabeth decided. The next day she would write a letter to Alex Hummel. "Oh, Regina! You're wonderful!" she gasped, leaning forward to hug her friend. "Maybe there is a chance, after all!"

Will Elizabeth leave Sweet Valley to study in Switzerland? Find out in Sweet Valley High #38, **LEAVING HOME.**

☐	27567-4	DOUBLE LOVE #1	$2.95
☐	27578-X	SECRETS #2	$2.99
☐	27669-7	PLAYING WITH FIRE #3	$2.99
☐	27493-7	POWER PLAY #4	$2.99
☐	27568-2	ALL NIGHT LONG #5	$2.99
☐	27741-3	DANGEROUS LOVE #6	$2.99
☐	27672-7	DEAR SISTER #7	$2.99
☐	27569-0	HEARTBREAKER #8	$2.99
☐	27878-9	RACING HEARTS #9	$2.99
☐	27668-9	WRONG KIND OF GIRL #10	$2.95
☐	27941-6	TOO GOOD TO BE TRUE #11	$2.99
☐	27755-3	WHEN LOVE DIES #12	$2.95
☐	27877-0	KIDNAPPED #13	$2.99
☐	27939-4	DECEPTIONS #14	$2.95
☐	27940-5	PROMISES #15	$3.25
☐	27431-7	RAGS TO RICHES #16	$2.95
☐	27931-9	LOVE LETTERS #17	$2.95
☐	27444-9	HEAD OVER HEELS #18	$2.95
☐	27589-5	SHOWDOWN #19	$2.95
☐	27454-6	CRASH LANDING! #20	$2.99
☐	27566-6	RUNAWAY #21	$2.99
☐	27952-1	TOO MUCH IN LOVE #22	$2.99
☐	27951-3	SAY GOODBYE #23	$2.99
☐	27492-9	MEMORIES #24	$2.99
☐	27944-0	NOWHERE TO RUN #25	$2.99
☐	27670-0	HOSTAGE #26	$2.95
☐	27885-1	LOVESTRUCK #27	$2.99
☐	28087-2	ALONE IN THE CROWD #28	$2.99

Buy them at your local bookstore or use this page to order.

☐	27590-9	**BITTER RIVALS #29**	$3.25
☐	27558-5	**JEALOUS LIES #30**	$3.25
☐	27490-2	**TAKING SIDES #31**	$2.99
☐	27560-7	**THE NEW JESSICA #32**	$2.99
☐	27491-0	**STARTING OVER #33**	$2.95
☐	27521-6	**FORBIDDEN LOVE #34**	$2.99
☐	27666-2	**OUT OF CONTROL #35**	$2.99
☐	27662-X	**LAST CHANCE #36**	$2.95
☐	27884-3	**RUMORS #37**	$2.95
☐	27631-X	**LEAVING HOME #38**	$2.99
☐	27691-3	**SECRET ADMIRER #39**	$2.99
☐	27692-1	**ON THE EDGE #40**	$2.95
☐	27693-X	**OUTCAST #41**	$2.95
☐	26951-8	**CAUGHT IN THE MIDDLE #42**	$2.99
☐	27006-0	**HARD CHOICES #43**	$2.95
☐	27064-8	**PRETENSES #44**	$2.99
☐	27176-8	**FAMILY SECRETS #45**	$2.99
☐	27278-2	**DECISIONS #46**	$2.99
☐	27359-0	**TROUBLEMAKER #47**	$2.99
☐	27416-3	**SLAM BOOK FEVER #48**	$2.95
☐	27477-5	**PLAYING FOR KEEPS #49**	$2.95
☐	27596-8	**OUT OF REACH #50**	$2.95

Buy them at your local bookstore or use this page to order.

━━━━━━━━━━━━━━━━━━━━━━━━━━━━━━━━

Bantam Books, Dept. SVH2, 2451 South Wolf Road, Des Plaines, IL 60018

Please send me the items I have checked above. I am enclosing $＿＿＿＿
(please add $2.50 to cover postage and handling). Send check or money
order, no cash or C.O.D.s please.

Mr/Ms ━━━━━━━━━━━━━━━━━━━━━━━━━━━━━━

Address ━━━━━━━━━━━━━━━━━━━━━━━━━━━━

City/State━━━━━━━━━━━━━━━━ Zip ━━━━━━━

SVH2–7/92

Please allow four to six weeks for delivery.
Prices and availability subject to change without notice.